secrets of my HOLLYWOOD LIFe
on location

a novel by

Jen Calonita

po

LITTLE, BROWN

New York

Also by Jen Calonita:

SECRETS OF MY HOLLYWOOD LIFE
and
SECRETS OF MY HOLLYWOOD LIFE
FAMILY AFFAIRS

Poppy

Little, Brown and Company
Hachette Book Group USA
237 Park Avenue, New York, NY 10017
For more of your favorite series, go to www.pickapoppy.com

First Paperback Edition: April 2008
First published in hardcover in 2007 by Little, Brown and Company.

The Poppy name and logo are trademarks of Hachette Book Group USA.

Library of Congress Cataloging-in-Publication Data

Calonita, Jen.
  Secrets of my Hollywood life : on location / by Jen Calonita.—1st ed.
    p. cm.
  Summary: Life is good for Hollywood princess Kaitlin Burke, ready to star in a movie by her favorite director, but an old love and a scheming new publicist complicate her already hectic existence.
    ISBN: 978-0-316-15440-6
  [1. Actors and actresses—Fiction. 2. Interpersonal relations—Fiction. 3. Hollywood (Los Angeles, Calif.)—Fiction.] I. Title. II. Title: On location.
  PZ7.C1346Shl 2007
  [Fic]—dc22
                              2006025293

10 9 8 7 6 5 4 3 2 1

RRD-H

Printed in the United States of America

Book design by Tracy Shaw

The text was set in Golden Cockerel and the display was set in Filosofia and Castine.

For the soon-to-be Mrs. John Neary,
aka my kid sister, Nicole

one: *The Comeback Kid*

The sound is unmistakable as it rises in decibel, frightening the blue jay that is drinking from the Italian marble bird-bath and causing our new landscaper, Joe, to drop his gardening hose. Only one thing could cause this much commotion on a beautiful, eighty-six-degree Saturday morning in Southern California — and it's not an earthquake.

"KAITLIN BURKE, YOU'RE BACK ON TOP OF THE HOLLYWOOD FOOD CHAIN WHERE YOU BELONG!" My publicist, Laney, loudly bursts through our living room French doors over to the pool area with my excited entourage in tow. Laney's pale blond hair, recently colored the exact shade she was born with, flies behind her as she strides ahead carrying a thick, glossy magazine.

It takes exactly two seconds for Austin and me to realize that we're being ambushed. He quickly jumps on the empty chaise next to me and tries to look like he's been busy worshiping the sun.

"What food chain? Were we supposed to have lunch

today?" I'm feeling disoriented from the marathon kissing session that Laney just interrupted. All I can remember right now is how good Austin's coconut-scented sunblock smelled when his face was nuzzled into my neck.

Laney must smell weakness because she stops in front of my chair and squints her dark-as-coal eyes at me. "What's wrong with you?" she asks suspiciously, pointing a ruby red manicured finger in my direction.

"Nothing," I lie, putting on my oversized black sunglasses to hide my guilty look that says, "I was making out with my boyfriend instead of memorizing lines."

My mom, dad, and younger brother are breathing down Laney's neck before my sunglasses are even pushed onto my nose. Matty pushes through the group and looks at the magazine in Laney's airbrush-tanned hands.

"That's what this is about? Another Kaitlin cover?" Matt rolls his emerald green eyes that match mine. "How exciting. NOT."

My best pal, Liz, would say Matty's being obnoxious because that's what thirteen-year-old boys do best, but I know the real reason he's been dissing me more than one spoiled socialite to another: Matty's itching to nail a part in the movie I just signed on to, which is currently known around town as *The Untitled Hutch Adams Project* (or as *Variety* dubbed it, "Hutch Adams's next surefire blockbuster"). I'm finally going to work with my favorite director, and the best part about it is that I can honestly say I like the plot. I play Carly Murray, a teen at an elite high school who finds out that she's been groomed since birth to become part of a shady super-human race. Matty is reading for the part of my younger brother. He's a shoo-in. I think so, our agent thinks so, and Hutch has alluded so, but Matt is practically menstrual over how long it's taking them to sign him.

"This is not just any cover. This is your *Fashionistas* cover!" Laney's smoky voice explains as she flashes the fashion magazine in Austin's and my face. On the front is a serious, or what some would call sexy, picture of me wearing a skimpy silver tank top, bikini bottoms, and Jimmy Choos. I'm sitting cross-legged with my bare arms wrapped around my chest. A ton of makeup (very unlike me) accents my face and my long honey-colored hair is wild, overblown with curls and piled high on my head, as only a high fashion magazine would request. Next to my picture in silver letters it says:

"My life was spiraling out of control and I knew I had to be daring if I wanted to fix it."
Kaitlin Burke: Confessions of the Comeback Kid

My mother-turned-business manager (who could pass as my twin after an hour in a makeup chair) squeals with de-light as she pushes past my beefy bodyguard, Rodney, and my assistant, Nadine, to squeeze onto the chaise on the other side of me.

"You see, Katie-Kat? I knew this town would forget what happened!" Mom shakes her highlighted hair and gives me a light hug, trying not to wrinkle the cream-colored silk cami that she's paired with ripped Earl Jeans. (My mom has traded her PB & J Couture sweat suit obsession for jeans in every brand, color, and style.) "Oh, hi, Austin," Mom adds stiffly, glancing over my shoulder. "I didn't know you were here."

My boyfriend of exactly four weeks, two days, and fourteen hours (but who's counting?) blushes a violent shade of fuchsia while I try not to grin. For once, I have to agree with Mom — landing *Fashionistas*, the most coveted magazine cover of all, is a big deal. My TV show *Family Affair* may be a ratings cow and *Entertainment Nation* may have named me "Teen Most Likely to Win an Oscar Before She's 30," but six months ago, Laney couldn't have booked me *Fashionistas* even if she begged, borrowed, and stole enough Ebe bags for the whole staff.

Nadine pries the magazine from Laney's grip. "'The comeback kid,'" Nadine reads aloud as she plays with her short, strawberry red hair. "This is a comeback? Please, you were only on the outs for a month!"

Sometimes I think Nadine is wiser than Yoda. Nadine hates Hollywood, which is why she and Austin are the perfect people to give me a sometimes urgently needed reality check. Raised in Chicago, Nadine doesn't hide her plan to use the money she's earned with me to go to business school so she can become the first U.S. female prez. I'm dreading the day she finally makes good on that threat. After three years, I don't know what I'd do without her running my schedule and, well, my life.

Laney squints menacingly at Nadine. "Maybe you've forgotten what a hideous month the last one was." She rummages in her white leather tote for her cell phone, which hasn't stopped ringing since she set foot on the poolside bluestone.

Just a few months ago, Casa Burke was bleaker than a visit to the Death Star. Worn out from my hectic shooting schedule playing fraternal twin Sam Buchanan on *Family Affair* and desperate for some privacy, I hatched a scheme with Liz for me to escape to high school for a few months of normalcy. But when you're paparazzi bait at Whole Foods, the only way you can pull off something that daring is to do it in disguise.

So I did, posing as a nerdy British exchange student named Rachel Rogers so that I could do crazy things like eat fattening fries in the cafeteria and crush on guys who didn't care how much my most recent movie made opening weekend. (Leave it to me to fall for Austin, who was seriously taken.) Things were actually going okay until my highly competitive *FA* costar Sky Mackenzie stole my Sidekick and read about my double life. Faster than you can say Mango-a-Go-Go (my favorite Jamba Juice concoction), Sky exposed me at a school dance in front of numerous camera crews. Liz and I think Sky tried to ruin me because she assumed the Teen Queen spotlight would pass to her while I would be banished to the D-list and offers from *Dancing with the Stars*. But Sky miscalculated.

Okay, to be honest I wasn't far from that fate when Laney and my family snapped me out of the yoga-like trance I'd retreated into. They convinced me to fight back with a media blitz in which I explained with almost embarrassing honesty that my disguise was a chance for me to be a regular teen. Within two weeks, the positive press was so redeeming that I secured the lead in Hutch Adams's untitled action flick (over Sky, who was also in the running) and accepted the *Fashionistas* cover that was originally supposed to feature fellow "It" girl Becky Callow. I also started dating Austin, who had recently dumped his cliquey cheerleader girlfriend, fallen for "Rachel," and eventually agreed to take a chance on the real me.

Even Hollywood couldn't come up with a screenplay that good.

I feel Austin's warm hand squeeze mine and my intense memories fade.

"Congratulations," Austin says softly, his tropical ocean-blue eyes dancing as they gaze into mine. It feels like 1,000 volts of electricity are pulsing through my fingers. A few weeks of pool time at my house have lightened Austin's growing blond hair, which now falls over his eyes. His red surfer-style swim shorts show off his lacrosse-toned arms and tanned abs. "I think that cover is cause to celebrate." He flashes his even white teeth. "How about dinner tonight?"

"Dinner is a great idea," my dad booms, obviously listening in with his free ear. His other one is on the phone setting up his golf tee time for Rancho Park Golf Course. His golf tee and khakis, along with sunglasses perched atop his blond head, gave it away.

Mom nods eagerly. "Nadine, see if you can reserve a table for all of us at Koi."

Before I can protest, Nadine begins dialing the silver Motorola I re-gifted to her.

"Done," Nadine announces a few moments later, snapping the cell phone shut and writing the change to my schedule in her leather folder, which we dubbed "the Bible" because it has all my personal info inside. "Eight o'clock at Koi, party of six." She smoothes the faded jeans and pink breast cancer awareness tee we both got at a benefit last week. "I thought you might want to invite Liz."

I nod. Well, I guess if everyone is coming. . . .

"Perfect!" Mom jumps up from my lounge chair. "I'm off for a treatment at Face Place. Jessica and Ashlee's mom is meeting me there." Before she takes two steps in her Kate Spade pumps, Mom notices my unopened script and frowns. I've been carting it around in the large white and multicolored Louis Vuitton agenda she gave me when I won the part. It's lying on the ground, next to my chair, and may have absorbed a little pool water. "You might want to run through lines with Matty this afternoon, Katie-Kat," Mom says coolly, raising her right eyebrow at me. "You've got a table read on Wednesday."

"I'm ready, Mom," I assure her.

"I've got to go too." Laney snatches *Fashionistas* back from

Matty, who is thumbing through it, probably looking for their occasional artsy topless model fashion spreads. "I have to meet Uma at Il Sole for lunch." She stuffs the issue in her bag and hurries back into the house. Like cattle, everyone else moves to follow.

Nadine spins around. "Kates, don't forget — four o'clock wardrobe fitting."

"Four," I repeat, fumbling for my relatively new Sidekick 3, which is covered in Swarovski crystals. Laney bought me the Sidekick 2 after Sky stole my original one, but when the newer model came out a month later, she promptly upgraded me again. ("You can't walk around with last year's version," she said dismissively when I claimed the 2 had more than enough gadgets for me to handle.)

When the French doors slam shut, it's so quiet you can hear the pool jets. Austin and I are finally alone again — well, if you don't count Joe, who is standing behind the rosebush with his pruning shears in hand and a bewildered look on his face. Good thing Laney left. I know she'd think Joe was spying on us for the tabloids.

"Where were we?" Austin creeps back onto the teak wood chaise and kisses me again. My stomach does a series of somersaults like it does every time Austin's lips are on mine. I can't help thinking how good it feels to be me for a change. Here's a guy who's not intimidated by my job, my family, or even my over-caffeinated publicist.

This leads me to the first of many new Hollywood secrets that I'm dying to divulge. HOLLYWOOD SECRET NUMBER ONE:

When it comes to celebrity dating, many stars talk about the benefits of dating a fellow actor. They reason that only someone inside the biz could understand when you work such grueling hours or collect a paycheck for playing a spelunker in peril. Between you and me, that "celeb-only" dating speech is week-old baloney. The truth is, it's *tough* to date a fellow actor. There's too much competition over who's the bigger star and too much stress over spending six months apart when you ship off to shoot a movie in Bangladesh and he is on location in the West Indies. The real reason why actors so often date other actors? We've got nobody else to date! Stars mostly spend time with other stars (and reality show hangers-on). A famous actress is unlikely to find her next relationship while pumping gas at the local Mobil.

That is, unless . . . you spend a few months pretending to be someone you're not. That's how I met a real guy like Austin. Now I just hope he can handle living under a microscope.

I kiss Austin's chin, then reluctantly lean away so I can look him in the eye. "Can we talk?" I ask nervously.

"Now?" Austin laughs. I nod and pull my longish legs and gargantuan feet up into a ball so that I can put a little space between us. That's the only way I can get through this conversation without reaching over and kissing him again.

"These past few weeks have been amazing," I start slowly.

"I know." Austin draws an imaginary circle on my knee, giving me goose bumps.

"I think you're vying for Boyfriend of the Year." Just last

weekend, Austin surprised me with my first trip to the circus and took me to Santa Monica Pier to try a corn dog. Since my film training sessions have been in the morning, and production meetings have been few, I've had my afternoons free to hang with Austin after he finishes lacrosse practice. Mom thought a few weeks off would leave me bored, but I'm cherishing every minute of freedom I have till filming officially begins. "I still can't believe they have go-cart racing in the Valley," I add out loud.

"Don't forget — you owe me a rematch, Burke," Austin teases. "I would have beat you if Larry the Liar and Sam the Slug hadn't set off flashes in my face."

"You remembered their names." I'm surprised he recalled my most persistent shutter hounds. "I'm impressed, Meyers." Austin's the only one who doesn't call me one of the million Kaitlin nicknames — Kates, K, Katie-Kat, Katie-Kins . . . take your pick — that everyone from my family to strangers on the street use. When Austin calls me "Burke," I feel like a completely different uncomplicated person that only he knows. It's exhilarating. I've started calling him by his last name too.

"But that's kind of what I wanted to talk to you about," I reply. "My free time is going to be scarce once I start Hutch's movie. And our start date is only two weeks away." As if either of us needs reminding.

"You'll be busy, but I have a lot on my plate too." Austin sounds a tad defensive. "Final exams are coming up and we made the division lacrosse finals. I told you what a bruiser Coach Connors is. Practices are going to be twenty-four-seven. Plus I'm coaching peewee lacrosse when school ends. I'm going to be pretty tied up myself." Austin's hair falls over his eyes and I can't read his expression.

"I just thought we should have a State of the Union before both our lives get crazy," I say hurriedly. "Once I get on set, who knows what will happen. Call times get bumped, my work schedule will constantly change, and I'll have appearances to make. But I'm sure I'll be able to bring a guest to most of them," I add.

"I'm not going to lie — sometimes I think it's surreal that I'm dating the famous Kaitlin Burke," Austin confesses as his cheeks turn as red as his swim shorts. "I guess that's why I'm nervous about going to events with you. This celebrity world of yours is a bit overwhelming." He smiles sheepishly, revealing the dimple by his left cheek.

"Mingling with other celebrities is the same as hanging with me," I promise, and lay a hand on his wrist. "Most stars are quite normal."

"If you say so." He doesn't look convinced. "But as far as your nightmare datebook, I get the picture." He shrugs. "I knew this wasn't going to be cake when I showed up at your compound a few weeks ago and said we should give this a shot."

"You're right." I bat my green eyes at him, hoping I look cute in this harsh sunlight, hoping the image of me in this teal bikini is enough to make him remember his words a month from now when the only time we have to see each other is 3 AM for a very, very early breakfast.

"I told you, all I ask is that you be honest with me." Austin's voice is soft and quite serious. "The one thing I can't stand is being lied to." He wraps his arms around my knees and rests his chin on them. "As for the rest of the Hollywood protocol, you can teach me as we go along. Sound good, Professor Burke?"

"Works for me." I kiss him softly on the lips. "That means I can give you this present." I blindly reach under the lounge chair and search for the small box wrapped in shiny silver paper that I planted there early this morning. I pull away from Austin and put the box between us. Austin takes it and tears the wrapping curiously.

"A Sidekick?" he laughs.

"This way we can talk anytime we want without interruption," I explain as he opens the box. "I can e-mail you when I'm waiting to shoot a scene and you can text me before class. These babies are quick."

"Thanks." Austin blushes. "But I feel weird about you buying me something so expensive —"

"Don't," I interrupt. "It's one of the perks you're going to have to get used to. And believe me; this gift is purely selfish on my part, Meyers." I flash him a toothy grin.

"Whatever you say, Burke." Austin pulls me close and we begin to kiss again. The familiar scent of coconut is enough to make me forget all about Hutch Adams, my lines, or my wardrobe fitting . . . for the moment.

Later, when Austin's left and I've stopped questioning how I lucked out in getting the greatest boyfriend in the world, I whip out my Sidekick to send myself a few reminders.

SATURDAY 6/2
NOTE TO SELF:

Sunday schedule
6 AM — Capoeira martial arts session — HOME w/ Paulo
7:30 AM — stretching w/Cirque du Soleil gymnast
MEMORIZE LINES!!!

***Movie Start Date: Monday, June 18

TWO: *Walk Down Bad Memory Lane*

"The forecast for Los Angeles is downright gloomy," The meteorologist says on the car radio as Rodney maneuvers through traffic towards our meeting at Wagman Brothers Studios. "Rain will be heavy at times so watch out for flash flooding. There's no doubt about it, kiddies — hunker down and stay inside today."

Hmm . . . even if inside means trapped in a Town Car with my bickering team?

"Watch it," Laney snaps as the car lurches forward and Nadine bangs into her, sending Laney's lipstick flying out of her hand.

Nadine ignores her. "Rodney, how much longer?"

"I don't know. The freeway is crawling," Rodney explains in between sips of his chocolate protein shake. "At this rate, we won't make it to Wagman's till 11:30, *if* we're lucky."

Nadine looks at her trusty plastic Timex and sighs loudly. "I wouldn't be in such a hurry if someone didn't stop at Lisa Kline to buy a sequin halter top," she mumbles.

I watch Nadine hastily punch some numbers on her cell phone. "Hi, Bernadette, it's Nadine," she says in a fake pleasant tone. "Nasty weather today, huh? Really, you were too? I'm stuck in traffic myself with Kaitlin Burke. I know. We'll be there as soon as we can." When Nadine hangs up, the silence in the car is so awkward that I concentrate on listening to the windshield wipers working furiously to keep up with the monsoon outside.

"I don't know why you're in a tizzy," Mom finally says as she flicks a stray thread off the boot-cut Blue Cult jeans she's wearing with a flowing orange silk shirt and leopard heels. "Lindsay's mom said this was the sale of the century and I couldn't miss it. You should have bought something yourself. Besides, it was a quick stop," Mom adds. "We were already on Robertson Boulevard."

"I just hope we aren't late to Kaitlin's meeting with Hutch and Carol." Nadine scratches her right eyebrow nervously. "I've heard stories about Carol Ingram. She may be new to Wagman's, but she was an A-list personal publicist for years before she made the move to studio marketing. Tell them, Laney. You worked for her."

"You did?" Mom, Rodney, and I practically say in unison.

Laney looks like she might open the back door and toss Nadine out into the storm. A rumble of thunder claps over our heads.

"I heard she was your mentor," Nadine squeaks while her face turns as red as her hair.

Laney looks out the fogged windows of the Lincoln

Rodney always chauffeurs us around in and sighs. "That was a long time ago," she says wearily. "I'm quite successful on my own, if you haven't noticed."

"We're moving!" Rodney interrupts excitedly, smacking the steering wheel. "There was a car with a flat tire in the left lane."

"But you know Carol's secrets, right?" Nadine prods Laney. "When Kaitlin signed on to Hutch's movie, I did some research on Wagman and found a scathing article about Carol in *New Money* magazine. It said she had Ace Makar banned from making movies at her last studio because he gave her trouble at a press junket."

"That's ridiculous," Mom says skeptically. "What head of marketing has that much power?"

"Carol's liquid gold," Laney explains sourly. "The last ten — TEN — movies she ran the publicity for made millions for Sonic Studios! That's why Wagman paid such a pretty penny to steal her." Laney looks away. "If only the deal could have happened after this movie," she mumbles under her breath.

"I've never heard you mention her before," I note curiously.

"We had a falling out when I left the private firm she ran." An unfamiliar pink tint spreads across Laney's cheeks. "I took some of her big clients with me."

"Ouch," Nadine sums up with a full-on grin. I think Nadine's mentally taking notes for her ascent of the political ladder.

"But that's all in the past," Laney says dismissively. "We've

crossed paths since then and always been professional."
Laney clears her throat.

Her words hang in the air-conditioned cabin. "This is exactly why I didn't want us to be late to this meeting," Nadine adds quietly, but not quietly enough for Mom not to hear.

"Don't get smart with me, Nadine," Mom snaps, clearly flustered by the Carol lowdown. "The meeting doesn't start till eleven thirty!"

UH-OH. I hear Rodney step on the gas and we ride the rest of the way in tense silence. As I watch lightning flash across the dark sky, I can't help but wonder about today's mystery meeting. Hutch has never scheduled a last-minute production pow wow. I wish I could say the move is classic Hutch, but I've only met with him a few times now and the rest I know from interviews — he's easygoing, loves to surf, and meditates on set when he's unsure of how to shoot a scene. I've heard through the grapevine his only drawbacks are that he's very secretive about scripts and is such a perfectionist that he sometimes falls behind schedule. I hope that doesn't happen with this film: I'm due back on *FA* in mid-August!

Hutch's producing partner Daniella Cook is the one I've been dealing with on a daily basis. She's been great. First she set up Capoeira (Brazilian martial arts) training sessions so I'll be in killer shape for the fight sequences. Then she hired a stunt coordinator from Cirque du Soleil to teach me how to fall out of a car or a window properly and got me classes with a dialogue coach to perfect a slight Irish accent, since my character supposedly spent part of her childhood in Ireland. She's also the one, along with my agent, Seth, who has been keeping me up-to-date on the flurry of script changes Hutch has been making (which I'll admit I'm not used to and am kind of nervous about). When Daniella hand-delivered the most recent version last Wednesday, she revealed that Hutch is getting his first screenwriter credit on this film. Daniella reminded me to guard the script with my life — Hutch has no tolerance for plot leaks.

Before I know it, Rodney has zipped through tight security and pulled up to the parking lot outside the plain brick Building 27 on Wagman's backlot. He jumps out of the car with an oversize umbrella in his hand and rushes around to the back to open the door for the rest of us. It's so windy, Rodney, who is six foot two and almost three hundred pounds soaking wet (like he is now), is getting banged around. He steadies the umbrella over the open drenched door and gives me a wink as rain pours down on his bald head.

"Let me worry about Carol," Laney growls at us as she slides out of the car first. "You three worry about why Hutch called this meeting in the first place."

My stomach flip-flops as the rest of us step out of the car, huddle under the umbrella, and make our way to the lobby. Daniella mentioned Hutch liked surprises, but I know the meeting can't be about him hiring Matty. We got that call from Seth yesterday and celebrated with a sushi dinner last night. Hmm . . . what is this meeting about???

OH GOD. MAYBE I'M BEING FIRED!

HOLLYWOOD SECRET NUMBER TWO: Just because *Variety* announces you snagged the role of your life in an upcoming film doesn't mean you're guaranteed to set foot on the production. Stars drop out of movies all the time, both voluntarily — boxing rehearsal injury, didn't like the latest script changes, got pregnant — and involuntarily — like when a director sees the error of his ways and realizes his lead isn't worthy. I know this mega-hot actor who had *two* hit TV shows and practically the pick of any upcoming movie he wanted. He signed on to do this big, I mean BIG, movie with a hot director and then was quietly dropped a few weeks before production began. Rumor has it the director realized his would-be leading man may be funny, but he so can't do serious drama. Gulp. I wonder if Hutch had a change of heart about *me*.

Once we're in the lobby and shake the rain off our jackets, I take a deep breath and look down at my sensible shoes. They're adorable gold Prada ballet flats that make my feet look small with the jeans and lilac Stella McCartney turtleneck sweater I'm wearing under my white Roberto Cavalli trench coat. I thought it was important to dress older and wiser today so that Hutch doesn't think he made a mistake hiring a sixteen-year-old to play a sixteen-year-old in his mega-budget action movie. Let's be honest: how many stars in this town actually play parts their own age?

OH GOD. I AM BEING FIRED! I feel myself start to hyperventilate.

"Are you alright?" Nadine asks.

I nod. There's no reason to break the bad news now, and anyway, my throat has constricted too much for me to utter more than a choked gasp. I follow the *click-clack* of Laney's and my mother's heels past the perky receptionist listening to Celine Dion and up the dark blue vinyl-covered stairs to the second floor conference room. Lining the bright white walls are several Wagman film posters and I pause to look at one of Hutch's, *Seeing Is Believing*. It's a giant picture of a beige metal blind that a sweating Jack Vitano is suspiciously peering through as Nicki Neary huddles in fear behind him. I love that film.

Please tell me my name will be in size 60 Helvetica font on the top of Hutch's next poster! I promise if it is, I'll be nicer to everyone I know, including Sky.

Mom is the first one through the conference room door. "See?" She chirps half a second later as she whips around to face Nadine. "No one's here yet." Nadine breaths a sigh of relief.

Shaking slightly, I walk into the large room. It doesn't resemble the typical conference room setup, which is a long table lined with swivel chairs. This room has huge windows that overlook Wagman's rain-soaked backlot, several aged brown leather couches, plush green suede recliners, and a large plasma TV. In front of each couch are mission-style oak coffee tables with binders stacked on them. I walk over to the nearest table and pick one up. Written in bright red ink on the front of the blinder is, "FOR YOUR EYES ONLY:

The Untitled Hutch Adams Project." I sink into the nearest recliner and feel myself start to decompress. It's not like Hutch would leave something as top secret as the new version of the script lying around if I wasn't still the star of the picture.

"Did I give you permission to touch that?" A gruff voice demands. I spin around, dropping the binder loudly on the plush almond-colored carpeting.

"GOT YA, Katie Bear," Drew Thomas, my movie costar, yells. I grimace at the familiar nickname. "Miss me?" Drew flashes his trademark ultra-white toothy grin with the confidence of someone who's seen hundreds of girls melt like butter at the sight.

"You almost gave me a heart attack!" I clutch my chest and Drew laughs even harder. He opens his arms wide and *waits for me* to hug him. I want to vomit. He's GOT to be kidding.

Seeing Drew in the flesh makes me queasy. I knew this day would come, but I thought it would have happened a long time ago. Hutch didn't have the two of us screen test together, even though we're playing the romantic leads (I thought it was odd, but Laney said Hutch goes with his gut on casting, even if that means hiring someone, as she said, "much less famous" for my counterpart), and our table read isn't until Wednesday. That means today is the first time I've actually seen Drew since the night we broke up. Can I call it breaking up if we only went on half a dozen dates? It doesn't matter. Even if it was short-lived, the truth is, I fell hard.

I had seen Drew from a distance at parties and read about his rising film career. He had a knack for picking small parts that stuck out, like a daredevil leukemia patient in *Heartstrings*, but still hadn't found a role that gave him the fame he craved. But we didn't actually meet till Drew appeared on *FA* for a four-episode story arc last fall. He played Sam's hot Latino pizza delivery guy. I loved the episode when the two made waves because Sam showed up at the Summerville Hope Charity Ball with a seventeen-year-old high school dropout on her arm. Of course, this being *FA*, there was more than a class issue at stake. It turned out Ricky was quick with his fist and desperately in need of anger management counseling. Ashamed, he wound up leaving Summerville in the middle of the night without saying goodbye and writing Sam a letter about his unhappy childhood. It was Sam's first broken heart — and mine.

"You didn't think we were exclusive, did you, Katie Bear?" I remember Drew asked when I found him sucking face with Lila Tompkin. Drew had just wrapped his last episode and we were supposed to celebrate the ten-day anniversary of our first kiss at a KISS-FM concert. I was running late from the *FA* set that night and told Drew I would meet him backstage.

When I saw them liplocked, I walked right up to Drew and Lila without thinking. "How could you do this to me?" I stuttered naïvely, biting my lip to hold back the tears. "You said I was your world."

"You were! You changed everything for me, Katie Bear," Drew said, giving my right hand a squeeze as his other hand rested on Lila's shoulder. "If I hadn't been seen around town with you, I never would have gotten an audition with Brett Ratner. That's where I met Lila," he added, motioning to the tall, Asian beauty who was beaming stupidly. "She's in his next project. Besides, my *FA* part is over now. It's time for me to move on." His nonchalance contrasted with my trembling legs and dry as sandpaper mouth.

"You used me," I realized aloud, feeling stupid as I thought about the dozens of roses he had sent to my film premiere that we attended together, the serenade he treated me to in front of a packed restaurant at Mr. Chow's, and the passionate kisses he always pulled me in for when he saw the waiting paparazzi. Come to think of it, we'd never really spent time together in private.

"Katie Bear," he said. "This is Hollywood. You're supposed to use people. That's how you get places." Suddenly I noticed that his brown eyes weren't warm and soulful. They were glittering and calculating like a cobra.

That's when I slugged him and ran out of the Staples Center without looking back (it was quite a hike, let me tell you, especially in Gucci stilettos). I had Rodney take me straight to Liz's so that I could sob on her shoulder and nurse my throbbing punching hand while we watched *Legally Blonde*, about another woman scorned. Like Elle, I swore to change things. But in my case, it wasn't about winning back my man; it was about avoiding the trap of others who might use me for my fame. I hadn't dated anyone else till Austin.

I cringe at the sharp memories. Seeing Drew again is a lot harder than I thought it would be. I take a deep breath and exhale slowly. Okay, I'm a lot smarter and more confident now.

"Good to see you, Drew," I say stiffly, and give him a quick hug. But Drew holds on tight. When I manage to pull away, I can't help but stare. I'll admit it, Drew is still impossibly gorgeous. That tanned complexion, the black hair, his tall, buff bod . . . it's no wonder *Entertainment Nation* dubbed him the Latin George Clooney.

"You've missed me, I can tell," Drew coos. I snap out of my trance immediately. "I've missed you too. I never should have let you go, Katie Bear."

PLAYER! I want to scream. *You just want to hook up again to get more face time in US Weekly!* Instead I look at Laney and she motions for me to sit down. She's already lectured me about being nice to Drew to avoid any publicity nightmares. Drew takes my silence as a good sign and plops down on the leather couch next to me.

"Missed doesn't describe what I'm feeling," I hiss through gritted teeth. But before I can say anything else, the Coach satchel I bought at their charity dinner this spring begins to vibrate. I grab it and eagerly pull out the Sidekick.

WOOKIESRULE: Guess who?

My heart catches in my throat. That *Star Wars* screen name is pure Austin!

Drew watches me curiously, his deep brown eyes taking in my every move, and I smile nervously. "This will just take a second," I say, ignoring the loud sigh from Mom, who never understood why I stopped seeing Drew. ("You're young. You should date lots of boys — and this boy should be one of them. He's going places, Katie-Kins.")

> PRINCESSLEIA25: Do I know U?
> WOOKIESRULE: BURKE! R U kidding me???
> PRINCESSLEIA25: LOL. U figured out how 2 work the Sidekick, huh Meyers?
> WOOKIESRULE: You're my first email. Like my screen name?
> PRINCESSLEIA25: Y.

Drew clears his throat. "Sorry." I try not to smile. Austin has that effect on me.

> PRINCESSLEIA25: Got 2 go. Mtg starting. TTYL?
> WOOKIESRULE: Y. May the force B w/you.

As I put the Sidekick safely back in my bag, Drew's team noisily enters the room and starts chatting with mine. I can hear Drew's publicist rattling off her clients' names to an unimpressed Laney. I look up in time to see Nadine leaving.

(She doesn't sit in on my meetings.) She crosses her fingers before disappearing.

"Making this movie should be fun, huh, Katie Bear?" Drew puts a hand on my knee. I quickly remove it. He reeks from musky cologne I don't recognize. He better not think he's wearing that stuff during our kissing scenes.

"Definitely. But you know that's *all* we're doing, right, Drew? Making a movie?"

"We were so good together," Drew protests. "How can you not want to try again?" I open my mouth to protest. "You can fight it all you want," Drew says with a wink. "That will just make my conquest more fun."

"Fight it? Are you crazy?" I whisper hotly. I'm dying to spill the fact that I have a boyfriend, but I hold back. Austin isn't ready to face the wrath of a Hollywood party boy who will stop at nothing to get what he wants.

For now, I have bigger things to worry about, like the fact that Hutch just walked in the conference room with a scowl planted on his face.

Yep, I'm convinced: I'm about to be officially unemployed.

THree: *Meet Cruella De Vil*

While Hutch's partner Daniella is all smiles as she enters the meeting room, Hutch looks positively grim. He pushes his long, dirty brown hair off his face to reveal dark bags under his eyes.

"Hello, stars," Hutch croaks as he takes a seat in the recliner next to Drew and me. He's wearing his classic uniform: a concert tee, faded denim jeans, and combat boots.

"Hutch, my man," Drew says, shaking our director's hand gruffly. "I'm looking forward to our start date. It will be good to work with my girl again." Drew gives my arm a squeeze.

"Did he just call me his girl?" I joke, trying to break the ice.

Hutch barely cracks a smile at either of us. He just leans back in the chair and stares at me with a frown on his face. I'm even more worried seconds later when I get my first glimpse of Carol Ingram, who enters the room just as a bolt of lightning flashes across the window.

The woman is practically a giant! Seriously, she must be

around six one, because she towers over everyone. As she stomps towards Hutch, Drew, and me in her knee-high black boots, Carol stares down the rest of the room. Even Laney looks nervous. With a long, pale face, short black hair, and a tight scowl on her thin, bare lips, Carol reminds me of a cross between Cruella De Vil and a vampire. Yep, one thing is certain: Carol looks the part of one of the most powerful women in Hollywood.

"You must be Drew," she says, shaking his hand. "You're just as handsome in person as you are on the big screen, and that's saying something." Drew laughs a little too loudly. I give him credit for being wise enough not to crack a comeback.

Next, Carol turns to me. "And Kaitlin. I've been dying to meet you," she says as she grabs my hand firmly and gives me a sly smile. I expect her teeth to be pointy. "You and I have *a lot* to talk about."

As Carol brings the meeting to order, I can barely hear what she's saying over the loud thumping of my strained heart and the rain hitting the roof of our two-story building.

"Hi, everyone, I'm Carol Ingram, Wagmans' new head of marketing. First of all, let me say how pleased I am that my first assignment as VP at Wagman is to work on Hutch's film." Carol flicks a speck of dust off her black power miniskirt. Everyone in the crowded room applauds, including Laney. "And I couldn't be happier that Kaitlin and Drew are the stars," she adds, upping the charm quotient.

Maybe I'm not getting canned? I can feel myself turning purple as I hold my breath in anxious suspense.

"We'll have no problem getting advance buzz on this picture with you two young, beautiful stars on board," Carol coos. "But of course, I'm just here to observe the artiste in action today. So now I'll turn the meeting over to Hutch." Carol smiles sweetly at my bored director before turning her attention back to Drew and me. "My office will be calling your people to talk about a production publicity tour," she practically whispers. "This is a new initiative here at Wagman, which I'll be starting with your film. I think you'll like it."

Did she just say production publicity? HOLLYWOOD SECRET NUMBER THREE: Most actors' film contracts detail their publicity requirements. While every star handles press differently — some will only do talk shows, some prefer print interviews, still others only talk to the foreign press — everybody is required to do something to promote the film they've signed on to. If you renege on that promise, it could derail your career. My girlfriend Lara skipped out of a European press tour due to "exhaustion." She hasn't been able to get a meeting with the studio, let alone the producer of the movie she screwed, ever since.

I've heard of directors like Peter Jackson allowing press on film sets, or keeping a production blog, but a production publicity tour is new to me. With such a hectic shooting schedule, how are we going to find the time?

"Thank you, Carol," Hutch says gruffly. "I'll keep this meeting short, as I'm sure my stars have plenty of work to do before we start production in two weeks. I know I do." I'm about to laugh, but I stop when I see Hutch's serious expression. "I actually called you all here to talk about a little surprise I have."

"Don't keep us in suspense, dude." I can hear tension in Drew's voice too. "Spill it."

"I've actually made some additional changes to the script that I think you'll all be pleased with." Hutch cracks a small smile. Before I nearly black out from fright, I notice the gap between his two front teeth. Hutch motions us to pick up the binders from the coffee tables.

I wonder how my role has changed now, if I'm even still playing it. My character's parents went from huge roles to supporting players, and my character Carly's best friend has been rewritten more times than I can count. Originally, Carly had an older sister who was a superhuman rebel; then the part was changed to a neighbor. In the last draft, Carly is betrayed by a scheming younger brother, which Matty just snagged. Please don't tell me they're doing away with Matty's part! It will crush him.

"Of course, the script alterations are nothing anyone in this room should be worried about," Hutch adds. "What I've tweaked does not affect the gravity of Drew's and Kaitlin's parts."

I'M NOT GETTING FIRED! I'M NOT GETTING FIRED!

THANK GOD! The pounding noise I've been hearing in my chest starts to fade and I flop limply in my seat.

"If anything, the addition of this third major character will beef up Drew's and Kaitlin's roles immensely," Hutch adds.

Third character?

"She was a minor player in the original script, but after this talented young lady auditioned for me, I couldn't get her out of my head," Hutch says. "While she wasn't exactly Carly, I realized she'd make a perfect Regina. With this sensitive, generous young actress filling the role, the play will be even more darkly ominous. I'm incredibly grateful for her insight on Regina's evolution. Thanks to her, I recognized that Regina instead of Carly's brother should betray Carly and Donovan."

Drew and I look at each other in a moment of solidarity. Who did Hutch hire?

"Drew, Kaitlin, I want you both to meet your characters' new nemesis." Hutch stands up and motions to the empty doorway. "Sky Mackenzie, you can come in now."

My heart starts throbbing again. Did he say SKY MACKENZIE???

Unfortunately, my hearing is fine because in walks my troublemaking *FA* costar in the flesh. At least I *think* she's Sky. Since our fiery last encounter after my Sidekick-stealing accusation, Sky's bleached her long dark locks white blond. Against her orange faux tan and her waif figure, the effect is both horrifying and mesmerizing at the same time. Sky struts across the room in hip-hugging cream fabric pants and a matching camisole. She perches on the arm of Hutch's recliner.

"Surprise, K." Sky shrugs her bony shoulders and giggles. A loud clap of thunder rattles the windows.

I don't know what to say, but I hope my mouth isn't on the floor. Whatever I'm doing, Sky is clearly enjoying watching me. That is, until she catches sight of Drew.

"Drew Thomas," she practically purrs. "We haven't met, but I know all about you. I'm a big fan." She extends her bony right hand, which has a shiny new Kabbalah string wrapped around her wrist. Drew takes her hand and kisses it, and Hutch actually laughs.

"See? They're meshing already." He appears happy for the first time today. Daniella nods approvingly.

"There seems to be some major changes here, Hutch," Carol interrupts as she scans the new draft. "We wrapped our radical publicity campaign around Drew and Kaitlin. How will this affect things?"

I'm confused. What's this radical publicity plan?

"Who's running this film, Carol, me or you?" Hutch snaps, not bothering to hide his anger. "Your publicity approach is still fine and Kaitlin, Drew, and Sky will do whatever you want them to do together or separately."

"But —" Carol begins again.

"My main concern, however, is making a movie that will kill at the box office." Hutch raises his voice. "These gorgeous kids are going to make us a seminal movie." He rises from his recliner and heads to the door. "Now if you'll excuse me, I have to look at a location on Encinitas for a chase sequence. I'll see you three at the table reading," he adds, and then he's gone.

Carol looks flustered. Without saying a word to any of us, she sweeps out after my director. Her harried assistant gathers her things and runs after her, returning a minute later. "Carol says goodbye," she squeaks over the sounds of Hutch and Carol bickering in the hallway.

With the bigwigs finally out of earshot, everyone starts whispering at once, reminding me of what happened at Clark High anytime a teacher left a classroom full of bored students alone for five minutes. Sky is flirting madly with Drew, which I take as a sign she's dumped our poor, sweet costar Trevor Wainright, who plays my boyfriend on *FA*. I dash over to talk to Daniella.

"Hi, Kaitlin," she says warmly. Daniella appears to be in her late thirties and has long, strawlike brown hair, which matches her tortoise-shell glasses. Today she's dressed in a simple button-down pinstripe shirt and dress pants.

"Hutch seemed kind of stressed," I understate. "Is he okay?"

"That man is like Jekyll and Hyde." Daniella leans in confidentially. "When he's not working, he's a peach, but when he's filming a project, watch out. He's a madman!" She laughs, but I don't see what's funny.

"Really?" I murmur. "I've never heard that about him before."

"Oh, you wouldn't read about his mood swings," Daniella says blithely. "We've done a pretty good job of making sure the press doesn't get wind of them. But don't worry, you'll get used to it. He makes up for his attitude problem with being brilliant behind the camera."

I smile weakly. "Thanks. I'll see you at the table reading." In a fog, I head to the door.

"Talk about typecasting a villain," Nadine whispers as I reach her in the waiting room. "I ran into Sky as she was waiting to be announced. I almost had a heart attack when I saw her! I just looked at your new script and Matty still has a part, thank God."

"Not in here," Laney reminds us both as she magically appears. She puts a hand on each of our backs and steers us towards the stairs. "PAULA, I'LL HAVE MY ASSISTANT CALL YOUR ASSISTANT TO SET UP LUNCH!" she yells back to Drew's publicist as Mom runs to catch up.

We don't get very far. Our path is blocked by a tall girl in Wrangler jeans and a purple velvet scoop-neck top.

"Excuse me, is Sky Mackenzie in there?" she says in a thick Southern accent.

"Yep. You can't miss her," Nadine says without skipping a beat. "She's the bleached blond who looks like a walking advertisement for rehab. She's flirting with the hotshot in the back."

The girl starts to cackle. Seriously, it sounds like a high-pitched cackle. With her poofy light brown hair and heavy red highlights, she looks like she just stepped out of *Steel*

Magnolias. I'm guessing she's about the same age as Nadine. "You must be Nadine," the girl says.

"How'd you know that?" Nadine demands.

"Because you're with Kaitlin Burke, of course." The girl stares as if Nadine were crazy. "This must be Laney Peters and Kaitlin's mama."

"And who would you be?" Laney asks coolly.

"Madison Taylor, Sky's new assistant." She holds her hand out to shake Laney's. I notice her nails are painted a bright chipped red. "Pleased to meet you, sugar."

"So Sky finally found a new assistant," I joke. Wait, did I just say that out loud? Madison smiles politely. "I know she's been looking for the perfect one *forever*," I add. Or should I say, since she fired her last one, three months ago. Sky went through four assistants last year, a record even for her.

"Yep, she found one," Madison answers without looking away from Nadine, who she is eying up and down. "I guess I'll be seeing y'all on set. Should be fun."

"Fun is definitely the right word if you're talking about Sky," Nadine says solemnly.

"MADISON? IS THAT YOU I hear? Get in here!" Sky barks.

Madison practically jumps. "Jeepers. I've got to go. Nice meeting y'all."

"Bye, Madison," I call as she runs into the conference room.

"Poor girl." Nadine shakes her head. "She won't last a week."

TUESDAY 6/5
NOTE TO SELF:

Read new script.
Wardrobe fitting @ 10 AM on Wed.
MOVE STUNT TRAINING TO 12:30 PM

**Table reading @ 3 PM on Wed.

A — Group A lacrosse final — 6 PM ON Wed.
Lunch w/Laney & Mom, Dad next Thurs., June 14

SCRIPT CONTINUED:

12 INT. CARLY'S KITCHEN - DAY
Setting is a slick, state-of-the-art kitchen with stainless steel appliances, minimalist decor, and cold, black granite countertops.

CARLY MURRAY, 16, and REGINA HALLOCK, also 16, and Carly's best friend, are in the kitchen making dinner.

REGINA
Okay, spill it. Why the sourpuss?

CARLY
It's nothing really. (pauses and looks at REGINA) Okay, this is going to sound silly, but do you ever wish we lived somewhere else?

REGINA
Lived somewhere else? Are you crazy? You hated Ireland. You said you had no real friends till you moved here. I remember you looked so pathetic on your first day that I had to ask you to sit at our table at lunch.

CARLY
Thanks a lot! No, you're right. Forget I mentioned it.

REGINA
We've got the sweetest deal of anyone I know – especially you – a hot boy toy, parents who give you anything you ask for, and a kick-ass car. What more could you want?

CARLY
I don't know. Sometimes things don't seem to fit, you know? My life is too perfect. Like a fairy tale. Don't you ever feel that way too?

REGINA
(laughs) Why would I? People would kill to be me.

CAMERA STOPS at REGINA, pans in tight on her face as she watches CARLY continue to cook. REGINA looks up at the ceiling, at something the audience can't see.

DONOVAN COOK, 18, strolls in wearing sweats. He's soaked from a heavy workout. He walks over to CARLY and kisses her. REGINA watches quietly.

DONOVAN
Tastes almost as good as if I made it myself. Hey, Regina. Staying for dinner?

REGINA

(hastily gets up from the barstool she's perched on)

No, I forgot I have some place I've got to be.

You guys enjoy.

FOUR: *Playing Hooky*

I fling the dog-eared script across my bed and pick up the phone on my cluttered bedside table. As I dial, I glance guiltily around my destroyed room. Green highlighters, large oak tag storyboards, and scribbled note cards with tricky dialogue are strewn everywhere. Our housekeeper, Anita, is going to kill me.

Liz answers on the first ring. "Hello?"

"It's me," I whisper. "I have to get out of this room. I've been memorizing lines all *day*."

"Are you saying what I think you're saying?" Liz's voice grows excited. "I *knew* you'd change your mind. This one is too good to miss."

I tap my fingers on the receiver and look from the script hanging off my bed to my door. "I think so." I bite hard on my already chapped lower lip. "Do you think I should ask Austin to go too? He's so nervous about Hollywood parties, but the longer he waits the more anxious he'll get. This party could be good practice because it's cool." I pick up a fluorescent green highlighter from my bed and pop the cap on and off. "Am I right? Or should I wait a bit longer before exposing him to the paparazzi blitz? I don't want to push him. Besides, he might not even want to come tonight. He had a grueling practice this afternoon and the coach yelled at him for talking during sprints. Maybe I should just stay home." I pause when I realize Liz hasn't said a word in ages. "Do you think I should just stay home?" I repeat blankly.

"RAMBLING," Liz says patiently. "Just call and ask him, okay? What boy can resist an Xbox 360 tournament? Who knows? Maybe he'll get to play *Madden NFL* against Carmen Electra."

God, I hope not. Who wants to compete with a girl who has topped *FHM, Maxim,* AND *Stuff*'s "Sexiest Women" issues? Not me. "Is Josh coming?" I ask to change the subject. Liz has her own invitations to this party since her dad is a lawyer for Xbox.

"Yep. He can't wait." Liz sounds giddy, like she always does when we talk about Josh. Or Austin. You'd think we'd never had boyfriends before. Well, okay I haven't had that many, but Liz has had plenty. "Come on, how much fun will it be for the four of us to go to a party together?"

I think it sounds awesome, but Mom isn't going to be happy about it. Principal photography starts in a little over a week and she wants me studying every waking minute even though Daniella told me I killed at the table read on Wednesday.

I really do need a study break. I've been working my butt

off between the daily three hours of training, accent coaching, and memorization. Thankfully, it hasn't been hard to get motivated. My character, Carly, is someone I'd totally be friends with. She's a take-charge kind of girl who is tired of being secluded from the regular world, like, well, like I was a few months ago.

I look at the door again. Even if I can sneak past Mom and Dad (not that I ever have before), what about Matt? Ever since he got the part of Carly's younger brother, Rob, last Sunday, he's been holed up in his room memorizing lines. If Matt comes looking for me and I'm not here, he'll rat me out for sure.

HOLLYWOOD SECRET NUMBER FOUR: I wish I could say there is a foolproof method to memorizing a script, but there's not. Every actor does it differently. I start by going through the pages and highlighting all my lines (in green, my favorite color). Then I reread my part to death. The key is to think about the meaning of the scene rather than just the words. When I do that, I can almost sense what the character's going to say next, even if I don't know the line verbatim. But the best help for learning a script is running lines with someone who will act it out with you. Rodney, who is itching to be an action star, is always game, as is Nadine, ironically. Sometimes they get so into their parts I have to pinch myself to keep from laughing.

If all else fails and you still don't know your lines, you can always hide out in your trailer till you've got the scene down pat or carry the script in a "book" and pretend to be reading the latest "it" novel. I'm not joking. I know many stars, myself included, who have pulled this stunt. But what am I worried about? I know my lines well enough. I'll only have to hide in my trailer if Hutch alters my dialogue for the umpteenth time.

"Okay, I'm calling Austin," I answer decisively.

"That a girl," Liz cheers.

We hang up and I hit number four on my speed dial (Liz is number one, then Nadine and Laney). Austin answers on the first ring.

"Guess who?" I ask.

"Hey, Burke." I hear his deep voice and I immediately melt. "Did your mom give you permission to call me?" he teases. "You're supposed to be studying."

He learns quickly. "I'm breaking out," I semi-joke. "Care to join me?"

"Where are we escaping to?" I imagine him curled up on his own disheveled bed, still wearing his lacrosse practice clothes.

"Well . . ."

"A work thing?" Austin asks, and clears his throat.

"It's an Xbox 360 tournament at the Mondrian and a lot of stars will be there. Xbox is previewing new games. Liz and Josh are going too," I explain.

This isn't just any Xbox party. It's a super-exclusive one that the company hosts from time to time just for their biggest supporters, meaning celebrities. My friend Justin, who is a major musician, is such a fan that the company actually threw him a birthday party one year and outfitted his house with several consoles for the bash. The Mondrian Hotel is a cool space for a party. In addition to booking the penthouse, Xbox reserved the Outdoor Living Room, which is a lavish deck overlooking the pool area. I'm sure the place will be packed to capacity as usual. At their last party, I beat my friend Wilmer and scored second place at *Halo 2*. (And Wilmer said girls stink at *Halo*. HAH!)

"Are you telling me I get to hang out with you *and* play video games?" Austin asks. "I'm sold."

My mouth breaks into a wide grin. Austin may be nervous, but I think he's ready for his Hollywood initiation. Before I can tell him that, there's a knock at the door. "Rodney and I will pick you up in an hour. I have to go," I whisper hurriedly, and hang up just as I hear the lock in my bedroom door begin to jingle.

I know immediately what's happening — Matt is busting in with a platinum American Express card again. When he gets the door open, he practically falls through it.

"Hey, Matty, what's up?" I grab the script hanging off my bed and pretend to be reading.

Matt looks exhausted. The white and brown striped button-down he's wearing with brown cords is rumpled and crooked. He eyes me suspiciously. "Were you just on the phone?"

He points to the receiver that's sticking out from my button-tufted taupe pillow shams. Darn, I thought I hid that.

I run my fingers through my messy hair. How am I going to explain this? "Uh, yeah, I was just talking to Liz," I answer, thinking out loud. "She was trying to convince me to go out tonight since I've been working like a dog."

He nods, his green eyes peering into my own. "I hope you told her no," he says seriously. "We should both be on our game when we start work next week. I think both of us should run lines while the house is quiet."

"Quiet?" I'm confused.

"Mom and Dad just left to meet the Hiltons at an Animal Rescuers auction at Shutters."

That's funny. Mom hates furry critters of any kind . . . WAIT. If Mom and Dad are out, they won't know I'm gone! Well, until the tabloid pictures appear in the glossies next week, but at that point I'll already be at work. I just have to convince Matty, who is going over our study plan.

". . . I'm actually quite fluent in the script, having studied it for almost a straight twenty-four hours. The goal is to run the script from start to finish three times. I'll read all the parts except yours. We'll stay up all night if we have to."

"That's a great idea, Matty," I gush. "But why don't we start tomorrow?" It is sweet of him to want to run lines. "Tonight I think . . ." — I hesitate, but I know it's the only way — "we should *both* take the night off and go out."

"OUT?" he stutters. His blond mop of hair almost stands on end. "We can't. Mom would never allow it." He fidgets nervously with the hem of his untucked shirt.

"She's not even home," I reply smoothly. "You need a break, Matty. We both do. I mean, once work starts next week, we're barely going to have time to eat cold China Fun let alone have a few hours a night to sleep. You're going to live and breathe that movie set."

"But I'm only in five scenes —" he protests.

I cut him off. "Yeah, but I know you. You're so dedicated to your craft, you're going to show up the rest of the time anyway, just to watch."

"That is true," Matty says to himself. He thumbs his own worn script uncertainly.

"So let's get out of here and party. Xbox 360 is having a bash at the Mondrian and we're *both* on the guest list," I lie. Well, it's not exactly a lie, since wherever I go, Matty is welcome too.

"Xbox?" Matty sounds interested. "Okay, but just for an hour."

I grin. An hour. It will take that long just to get through press. Hopefully Matty will have such a good time, he won't look at his watch.

Forty-five minutes later, after Mom and Dad have phoned in to check on our studying, and Rodney has happily agreed to help with our breakout, we pull up in front of Austin's brick colonial in Santa Rosita. I quickly double-check the makeup I applied in the back of the car and give my hair a final once over. I didn't have time to shower again, so I pulled my hair back into a low ponytail, slipped on a pair of Mom's Rock & Republic jeans, and grabbed a ivory lace tank I've accented with a black ribbon tied around my waist.

Austin opens the back door to the black Lincoln himself and peers inside. He looks cute in a button-down blue pinstripe shirt and dark denim jeans. "Hey, Burke," he says with a toothy grin. As he slides into the car, he does a double take when he sees Matt sitting on the other side of me, yakking on his cell. "Hey, Matt."

Matty just waves and keeps on talking. Austin looks at me with large, questioning eyes before leaning in for a kiss.

"Sorry," I whisper, motioning to Matty. "He was my alibi."

"Chaz, are you serious?" Matty groans. "I can't believe you're not on the guest list. I hear Mina Burrows is going to be there. You're missing out, dude." His wide smile quickly turns into a frown. "No, I'm not my sister's plus one!"

"It's cool," Austin chuckles as he puts his hand on my knee. "So is there anything I should or shouldn't do at this thing? Like not kiss you?" I love that he smells like fresh-cut grass tonight.

"You better kiss me!" I laugh. "Just be yourself." I have to admit I'm nervous about our first joint appearance together too. "And don't let anyone or anything throw you. A lot of the people you meet will just be trying to show off — who they know, where they've been last . . ." I trail off.

"Wow." He runs his free hand through his wet hair.

"What?"

"I'm just impressed that you've survived this long without becoming like that yourself," he says softly.

"DUDE, I'M ON THE GUEST LIST!" Matt barks. "I'm on my way there now! Too bad you can't get in. I'm telling you, this Hutch movie is doing wonders for my rep."

"Yeah, well, I have my ways of staying grounded." I wink.

In almost no time I hear Rodney yell, "Kates, Mondrian in three and a half." I look up and notice he's steering with one hand and eating an In-N-Out burger with the other.

"Three is code for the number of blocks we are from an event," I explain.

Austin clears his throat. I wonder if he's worried about the paparazzi. I grab the hand he has on my knee. Suddenly it feels clammy. "Just follow my lead," I reassure him as Rodney pulls up outside the hotel. A valet opens the door and Rodney tosses him the keys. After he lets Austin, Matty, and me out, Rodney steers us through the low-lit, minimalist, modern lobby. Rodney is a big fan of intimate events: without crowds to control, he can just hang back and enjoy the Thai chicken skewers after ushering me through the press line.

A slight girl in a black Xbox t-shirt and a headset sees us and waves us over. She checks her clipboard and points to the elevator. "Penthouse," she whispers, almost in code, so that other guests in the lobby can't hear her. "Burke plus two," she says into her mouthpiece. I notice Austin eye the white draped walls and Tim Burton-esque egg-shaped chair. I smile weakly. What if he hates my scene already?

When the elevator doors open at the Penthouse, we're greeted by a clone of the girl downstairs. Actually several people are milling about wearing the same black Xbox t-shirts and headsets. I can hear the laughter and music pumping outside.

"Hi, Kaitlin," one of the girls says with a thousand-watt

smile. "We're so glad you could join us. We've already reserved you a gaming area on the pool deck. If you wouldn't mind talking to the press before proceeding outside, we'd greatly appreciate it." I look at Austin and he nods nervously.

"Should I do press too?" Matty asks the girl.

"I'm sorry, who are you?"

Matt looks aggravated. "Matt Burke. One of the stars of *The Untitled Hutch Adams Project*."

"Oh, okay, go ahead." She motions to another girl wearing an Xbox shirt. "Tell the press that Kaitlin Burke *and* Matt Burke are next."

"Matty, you go first," I offer. He doesn't refuse, bounding ahead and practically knocking over the E! Online reporter stationed at the top of the stairs. Rodney shakes his head and follows behind him. I see three more interviewers lined up after the E! one, along with several photographers. This should take about fifteen minutes. I grab Austin's sweaty hand. "Are you ready?" I whisper. He nods slowly.

When it's my turn, I greet the curly-haired brunette with glasses from E! She immediately looks at Austin, and I panic.

"I'm Austin." He shakes her hand as he clears his throat again.

"Are you two together?" She looks intrigued and brings her tape recorder closer to my face.

"Yes, we are. Did you have any Xbox questions you wanted to ask me?" I answer nervously. "*Halo 2* is my current favorite," I add. The girl blinks rapidly. I think she knows I've shut down the invasive Austin questions.

Austin and I move on to the second and third reporters. Both ask how long we've been dating and I leave out how we met and what our favorite dates have been. I don't want to taint what we have by describing it. I'm constantly reminding myself that quotes live on forever. If I say Austin and I love going to the beach and three months from now we change our minds and I tell another reporter that we both hate the sand, they'll call me on it and think I'm lying. No, it's better to keep some details private. Sorry, *Hollywood Nation*.

I'm in the middle of describing the plot to Hutch's film (as much as we've been given permission to reveal) when I hear "KATIE BEAR!" Next thing I know, I'm being lifted by the waist into the air. I lose my grip on Austin's hand and flashbulbs pop like fireworks. When I hit the ground, after pounding on a pair of well-defined arms repeatedly, I turn to face my kidnapper. Rodney barrels over with a Thai chicken skewer in his right hand.

Of course, it's Drew. He's wearing a tight silk muscle shirt and fitted jeans. He shoulders Austin aside and puts his arm around me, turning me back to the reporter from *Hollywood Nation*. I motion to Rodney that I'm okay, but he hangs back with a scowl on his face. He's not a big Drew fan.

"How cute is my Katie Bear?" he plays up to the excited girl, who motions for her camera guy to get a close-up. "She's my costar in *The Untitled Hutch Adams Project*."

"They know that, Drew," I answer through clenched

teeth as I gingerly remove his tight grip. "I've already been interviewed. It's your turn."

Drew talks directly to the *Hollywood Nation* crew. "You guys probably want us to answer some questions together, right?" I turn around and look for Austin. He's stepped back and is standing next to Rodney. He's staring straight at Drew with a look of annoyance on his face. "I'm sorry," I mouth. He cracks a weak smile. "Two seconds," I add, thinking of Carol Ingram and her plea for production publicity. Hopefully a few questions with Drew will fit the bill.

Drew and I talk about the film again and I play the part of perky, adoring costar as well as I can, the whole time worrying more about Drew's hands, which keep creeping back onto my waist or over my shoulder, than about what I'm saying. After Drew suggests the nearest paparazzo snap a few shots of us together — Matty begs his way into one of them — we're finally through the press line. As soon as we're out of earshot of the reporters, Drew's over-caffeinated persona shifts into low gear.

"Can I get you a drink, Katie Bear?" he offers, his eyes trailing a willowy blond model walking past us.

"No, but you can come with me," I grab his arm and steer him over to Austin. As we approach, I try to size up Austin the way Drew will. Gap threads, a barber haircut . . . GOD, Drew is going to rip him to shreds. "Drew, this is my boyfriend, Austin." Against my will, my voice trembles.

Looking less than thrilled, Austin sticks his hand out to

shake Drew's. Drew eyes Austin up and down with a vengeful grin.

"Drew is my costar in Hutch's new movie," I add miserably.

Drew smiles slyly as he holds out his hand. "I didn't know you had a boyfriend, Katie Bear."

"That's because we didn't have a chance to catch up at the table read with all the script changes," I blurt out. My heart pounds.

Drew shrugs. "Whatever you say." He starts walking away backward. "I'll catch you later, Katie Bear. Nice meeting you *Arnold*."

"It's Austin," my boyfriend grumbles.

As soon as Drew is gone, I pull Austin over to the deck railing. It's romantic overlooking the Los Angeles skyline, but at the moment I need to do damage control. "Listen," I begin.

"Don't sweat it," Austin murmurs, taking in the scene around him. The deck is packed with beautiful people, many scantily clad, blond, and holding martini glasses. There are TVs set up in every corner where people can play the latest games and a DJ pumping tunes from a platform they've placed over part of the pool. "I've already got his number."

I exhale deeply.

"What was with him being all over you though?" Austin glares at the memory.

Rodney gives me a scolding glance. "If you don't need me, I'm going to head over to the buffet with Matty," he says gruffly. I ignore him and laugh nervously.

This is definitely not the right time to bring up my past with Drew. "Drew's like that with all girls. He's just your typical player."

"That's for sure," Austin adds dryly, still looking around. "He's going to be a great costar."

Austin's kidding, right? It's so hard to figure boys out sometimes. Thankfully Liz and Josh arrive seconds later to rescue me from awkward conversation hell.

"Hey, man," Josh says, shaking Austin's hand. Josh's strawberry blond curly hair is almost to his shoulders and he's wearing jeans and a red polo shirt that shows off his toned arms from the daily kickboxing classes he takes with Liz. That's where they met.

"A week and counting," Liz groans, referring to my movie start date. "I'm going to miss seeing you practically every day." She looks so pretty tonight in a pale blue peasant dress that accents her curves and looks great against her olive skin. "At least when we were in class together, I had someone to laugh with over Principal P's goofy morning announcements."

"You've only got a few more weeks of school," I remind her. "We're filming most of the movie in Los Angeles so when you're done with finals, you can hang out in my trailer with me every day like last summer. I need you to keep Sky off my back." And Drew. But I'll fill her in on that part later.

Liz grimaces. Her curly brown hair blows in the light wind and she pushes it off her face. "I've been holding off telling you this because I didn't want to stress you out, but I won't be on set much this summer."

"Why not?" I ask, surprised.

She rolls her dark brown eyes. "Daddy wants me to have a *job* this summer. Something about getting a taste of the real world." Josh and Austin burst out laughing.

"Poor you," moans Austin. "A *real* job." Liz frowns at him.

"You don't understand," Liz protests. "I've been on all of Kaitlin's summer shoots. I help her run lines, organize her fan mail, and bring her hot tea . . ."

It's true. Liz and I had the best time while I was shooting *Off-Key*. She was around so much people mistook her for Nadine!

"You're like my second assistant," I realize suddenly. "I should just pay you and then you wouldn't have to get a job."

"I don't need the money," Liz says dismissively. Liz's dad is loaded. He's the top entertainment lawyer for half of Hollywood, including me. He works at the same firm as Sky's dad.

"But that would get your dad off your back," I suggest excitedly. "And we'd still get to be together. On location, a lot of people have more than one assistant because there's more to do than just the regular stuff. I'm sure Nadine would love the help. And besides, you always said you wanted to learn about producing movies. When you're not busy, you could shadow Hutch's producing partner, Daniella Cook."

"You think so?" Liz taps her pale blue clutch thoughtfully. "I would like the chance to do that."

"And Rodney could pick you up on our way to the set and take you home so you wouldn't —"

"I think she gets the idea." Austin laughs, putting his hand over my mouth as a flashbulb goes off nearby. Great, I can just imagine the *Us Weekly* caption for that photo.

"I'm in." Liz grins. I grab her and the two of us jump up and down and squeal as someone takes more pictures. Josh and Austin look amused as they move back to give us room. In the middle of the commotion, Rodney and Matty walk over with plates piled high with Szechwan beef and lobster eggrolls. An Xbox girl with a clipboard follows them.

"Kaitlin, do you and your friends want to go over to your gaming area?" she asks. The four of us look at each other.

"Let's go," Josh suggests, looking at Austin.

Liz and Josh take the lead. I grab Austin's hand and, as always, feel comforted to hold it in mine.

"So you can pay Liz to hang out on set, but you don't want me around?" he asks.

My mouth drops. I didn't even think of asking Austin. "Of course I want you to visit. I just thought —" I gasp.

"I'm kidding." Austin chuckles. "It would be weird to be employed by my girlfriend. And besides, I think the less I'm around Drew the better."

My stomach twists. "I'm sorry about earlier."

"Forget about it," Austin says good-naturedly. "But if you *really* feel bad about it, I know a way you can make it up to me."

"How's that?" I ask.

He gives me a mischievous grin. "Is that Carmen Electra over there?"

I follow his gaze and see the beautiful brunette in a tight mini. "I think so," I reply meekly.

"If you could get me one game of *Madden* with her, I think I could forget all about Drew what's-his-name."

I guess that's worth seeing your boyfriend flirt with a professional model. "It's a deal," I say, trying not to sound jealous.

SATURDAY 6/9
NOTE TO SELF:

Movie starts in 1 week!!!
Accent class — 10 AM, Mon.
EW Interview — 3 PM, Tues.
Stunt training w/Drew — 6 PM, Tues.
Final Wardrobe fitting — Wed. 11 AM, after Capoeira session

*Lunch with Laney, Mom, Dad — Thurs. @ 1 PM, Wilshire's

FIVE: *Wilshire's*

It takes me almost ten minutes to drag my bruised, battered, and completely exhausted body from the curb in front of Wilshire's restaurant, where Rodney's dropped me off, to the patio. Every step is agony, and all I can think about is having Nadine book me a deep tissue massage after lunch. Maybe it's because principal photography's only four days away, but my already hardcore trainers have become ultra-hardcore, and this morning's sessions were *killer*.

I slowly wind my way around Wilshire's patio and scan the crowd of beautiful people for my parents and Laney. The organic eatery is one of Laney's new favorite restaurants. I'm not sure if the draw is the delicious food or the garden dotted with real fireplaces, candles, and canvas sails connecting one tree to the next, but the atmosphere here is serene even during a business meeting.

"Hi, Katie-Kat," Dad greets me as I approach the table. Mom and Laney are so deep in conversation, they don't realize I've arrived till Dad announces me. Mom quickly slides the magazine they were both looking at off the table and into her new Gucci tote.

"Hi, sweetie!" She sounds almost too happy.

"What was that?" I gingerly lower myself in the chair.

"Would you like a drink, Ms. Burke?" A cute blond waiter saves Mom from answering.

"Chamomile tea with honey, please," I request. "And make it a pot."

"Tough workout, Katie-kins?" Dad booms cheerfully. Suspiciously, I keep my eyes on Laney and Mom. "Well, they've got to get you souped up for this role," he adds. "Can't run an engine without oil, honey."

I nod, even though I'm not sure what Dad's hokey car speak means. Dad's a producer now (he usually works on my films, but he won't be on this one. Hutch usually sticks with the same producers on all his films), but the terminology lingers from his car salesman days.

"What's going on?" I demand as Mom and Laney begin whispering again. Laney opens her mouth to answer and promptly shuts it as our waiter appears again with my tea.

"Thanks." I gratefully pour some tea, then turn back to Laney, who is rapping her long nails on the table while she stares at me.

Oh I know! Maybe they're annoyed I didn't change my outfit. "I'm sorry," I apologize. "I didn't have time to go home and shower." I'm still wearing my eggplant-colored velour warm-up suit from stunt training and my hair hangs in a high, sweaty ponytail. Hey, but Dad's not dressed up either.

Though Mom and Laney are in pant suits, Dad's wearing his standard golf shirt and pleated khakis. Humph.

"It's not that, sweetie." Mom eyes me up and down. "Although it wouldn't hurt to leave an extra pair of jeans and a sensible blazer in the car for emergencies."

"Emergencies? What's happened now?" I groan, instantly feeling even more tired.

"I wouldn't say *emergency*," Laney explains hurriedly, narrowing her eyes at my mother. "More like an unexpected change in plans. Nothing you can't handle."

I don't say anything. I know from experience Laney will spill the bad news when she's ready. But before she can continue, her cell phone rings. She looks at me apologetically, then turns towards the glowing fireplace behind us. "*I told you, Beth*, hold my calls," she hisses. "Unless it's Reese. Or Russell. Or Julia." She snaps shut the razor-thin cell phone, a gift from Usher. "Your mom and I just came from a meeting with Carol Ingram and Drew Thomas's people," Laney explains after a long pause. "She outlined your pre-publicity requirements for *The Untitled Hutch Adams Project*."

"Is this movie ever going to have a name?" Dad asks as he mulls over the menu.

"Oh, is that all?" I thought something major happened, like Hutch wanting me and Sky to change roles. (I had that nightmare last night.) "Drew and I did some press together at the Xbox party last weekend. It wasn't so bad."

"See? She doesn't mind doing appearances with Drew." Mom nudges Laney. "Speaking of the Xbox party, I thought you were supposed to be studying Saturday night." Mom raises her right eyebrow.

I hide my head in my menu. Crab cakes, mouth-watering risotto, and vegetarian pasta. Hmm ... I have to wear a bathing suit for the swim meet scene we're shooting on Sunday. Maybe I should have a salad. When I close the menu, our waiter is waiting.

"I'll have the calamari and watermelon salad," I order. When the waiter leaves, I get down to business. "Let me have it."

Mom looks at Laney. "Let's talk about some good news, shall we?" Laney suggests. "Seth called this morning and said your film rider was approved. A NordicTrack elliptical trainer will be delivered to your trailer on Sunday."

HOLLYWOOD SECRET NUMBER FIVE: Film riders — those phantom documents that contain all of a celebrity's demands for a film, TV show, photo, or music shoot — are the icing on the status cake. A-listers typically have contracts that allow them 30 to 40 perk points, each of which involves some sort of financial compensation, like $1,500 a week for an on-set nanny or $1,000 a week for a trainer. I asked for an elliptical, which will not only help me stay fit for filming but also provide stress relief, and a supply of tea and Coffee Bean and Tea Leaf fat-free vanilla Ice Blendeds. Studios are used to the requests, but they still triple cross their fingers that stars' demands don't spiral out of control. I know a former costar who insisted on eight-hundred-thread-count sheets on her hotel room bed, $75 vanilla candles burning in the bathroom, and chilled raspberries on the nightstand *every night*.

"Your elliptical request was nothing compared to what Sky asked for," Laney whispers, sliding her Louis Vuitton shades over her eyes to block the bright sun. "In addition to completely organic meals, and Evian stored at a slightly chilled temperature, Sky demanded oxygen be pumped in her trailer to keep her refreshed."

Mom rolls her eyes. "Anyway, Seth also said to tell you that Liz has been added to your payroll and that the studio is going to pick up the tab."

"Wow, that's awesome!" My hungry eyes follow the waiter as he places a bread basket on the table. Mom catches me staring and raises her right eyebrow again. I wouldn't dream of taking a piece under her watch, even if it has been hours since Bruce made me a banana shake that tasted like chalk.

"Kate-Kate, next time you want to add an assistant you should talk to Nadine about it beforehand," Dad warns. "She was a little upset to hear that you were hiring Liz for the shoot."

"She was?" I thought Nadine liked Liz. "She's always so busy on my film shoots that I thought she'd welcome an extra pair of hands."

"You know Nadine," Mom says briskly and pushes her hair behind her shoulders. "She likes to take credit for doing all the work herself."

Dad clears his throat. "Honey, Nadine told me she's worried that she and Liz are too different to be your joint assistants. She doesn't mind Liz hanging out on set, but she said when it comes to a job, they have different ethics and backgrounds."

"Liz wouldn't be caught dead with a shopping bag from Discount World, if that's what Nadine means," Mom chides. Laney snorts.

I shoot them both a warning look. Discount World is one of those superstores where you can buy everything from dishwasher detergent to polyester blend clothes. Nadine loves their bargain finds. She got most of my school disguise clothes there. "She's not leaving me, is she?" I suddenly panic. "I thought she wasn't ready to apply to business school!"

"She didn't say she's leaving," Dad soothes me. "But talk to her about Liz, okay, sweetie?"

"The bottom line is you have two assistants this summer and you're going to have a great time shooting this movie," Mom throws in gushingly. I knew it! Something *is* wrong. Mom is too happy for a woman who is missing a great sale at Maxfields to have our lunch.

"There is one more thing," Dad inserts delicately. "The studio wouldn't budge on letting you use Paul and Shelly for hair and makeup."

I frown. Paul and Shelly have been with me forever on *Family Affair*. They're good company and I trust them completely, which is why I try to use them for all my work. They helped me come up with my high school look.

"Hutch has the same artists work on all of his films," Mom explains.

"It was a long shot," I say sadly.

"Now the less-than-great news," Laney says, putting her bony tanned arms on the table and leaning forward. "You're going to have to do *a lot* of press for this movie, Kaitlin, and when I say a lot, I mean A LOT."

"Okay." I shrug, reaching inside my bag for my whirring Sidekick. I pull it out and look at the message. It's Austin.

WOOKIESRULE: Hey. Miss U. I'm in Mrs. Desmond's and we're playing French hangman. What's the word 4 book? Le Book?

He's so cute.

"...and most of it is going to be done with Drew. Kaitlin?" Laney scolds as I type back.

PRINCESSLEIA25: It's le livre, Meyers!

"Drew, got ya." I giggle, not looking up.

"KAITLIN, THEY WANT IT TO LOOK LIKE YOU TWO ARE DATING." Laney spits out loudly.

"WHAT?" I screech, startling the poor waiter. My salad almost flies off my plate as he places it in front of me. "Carol wants us to pretend to date?" My heart starts racing.

"Now that I have your full attention, no, Carol didn't come out and *actually* say that," Laney back-peddles, "but I'm not stupid. I know that's what she was getting at by insisting you arrive at several major upcoming events together without dates. It's a terrible idea, but there's no arguing with her." Laney shudders. "You should have heard her: 'I'm trying to help your client, Laney.' Ha! I'm sure she's just trying to destroy me through you."

"Why would she want people to think we're dating?" I ask, clutching my Sidekick to my heart. What will the world — namely Austin — think if I start popping up everywhere with Drew? "I won't do it. I don't have to do anything that's not in my contract."

"Dating Drew is not in your contract, but unfortunately following Carol's publicity requirements is," Laney states. I look at Mom, who handles all my contracts.

"How could I know what Carol was up to? I thought any publicity for the film was good publicity." Mom nervously pats her hair, which is straightened.

"I don't get it. Why would she think us dating would help the movie? Whenever people hook up on set, it usually ends horribly," I remind them. "Couples break up and refuse to do post-production publicity together, and the bad blood is all over the weeklies."

"I almost think she's hoping you two fight in public," Laney says grimly. She seems quite calm, almost beaten, which is *so* not like her. "Carol doesn't think bad blood means bad publicity. She believes tabloid coverage is great free press. As long as it's juicy and not slanderous, then it helps create buzz about a film, whether the couple is real, fake, or broken up." Laney stabs a piece of cucumber with her fork.

"She wants to get people talking," Dad suggests. "It's not

such a bad idea, sweetie. It will keep both you and Drew in the public eye while you're off TV screens for a few months."

"Carol's approach is too aggressive," Laney counters. "The way to get a star good publicity is to have them do high-profile films, avoid excessive partying — which only leads to catfights and dark circles under your eyes anyway — and arrive on the red carpet looking drop-dead gorgeous."

Who knew Laney was so sensible? I've never been so grateful to have her as my publicist.

Laney raises her orange-tinted sunglasses and looks around to make sure no one is listening in. "Carol's philosophy isn't unheard of though," Laney whispers. "You won't find many in this town who would actually admit it, but there are people who believe staged romances help box office returns. I've heard the rumors for years about aging Hollywood stars signing contracts with young, beautiful ones who'll date them for a year to boost both their star appeal."

I let out an audible sob. "No one is going to believe that Drew and I are a couple," I insist. I bite my lip hard. "It's obvious I can't stand him."

"Yeah, well, not to everyone." Laney slaps the latest issue of *Hollywood Nation* on the table. On the cover is a picture of Drew throwing me in the air at the Xbox event, me smiling away, and next to it is a shot of Austin, alone playing lacrosse. How'd they get that? The headline says:

WHO'LL CAPTURE KAITLIN BURKE'S HEART? HOLLYWOOD'S NEW BAD BOY OR THE HIGH SCHOOL HEARTTHROB?

I flip to the story on page eight and scan it. Drew and I are costars, blah, blah, blah . . . "STOLEN MOMENTS WITH THE FAMED PLAYER WHILE AUSTIN STOOD GLUMLY IN THE CORNER." I read on. Xbox party, blah, blah, blah . . . "THE TWO DATED LAST YEAR."

OH MY GOD. Now I have to tell Austin about Drew!

Noooo. I can't do that. The breakup is still too painful for me to talk about, and this publicity plan . . . It's too complicated to get into. Austin will never understand why I have to go along with it. But if I don't tell Austin something, someone else will. Like Lori. Austin's ex was always hiding *Hollywood Nation* in her textbooks.

Okay, I know what I'll do. Austin doesn't need to know everything I do at work. It's a known fact stars have to do *some* publicity together. I'll just make it clear to Austin that the events will be minimal. Austin will understand that part. As for Drew's and my relationship, I'll just tell Austin we went out once or twice. My Sidekick whirs again.

> WOOKIESRULE: Nice, Burke. Can U meet 4 dinner? Slice of Heaven? U, me, and Rodney?

"Who are you e-mailing?" Mom demands. "Austin?" I nod. Mom turns to Laney and Dad as if I'm not sitting right next to her. "She spends more time e-mailing Austin than she does memorizing her lines."

"That's not fair," I counter, looking up from my Sidekick.

"You said that I could have more free time and this is how I want to spend it," I reason. "It's not like I'm neglecting my work." I push the Xbox party out of my mind. "I'm going to be working six days a week starting Sunday so I won't be seeing Austin as much as I am now. What's wrong with having a boyfriend, anyway?"

Mom purses her lips and Laney nudges her. "Nothing, I guess," Mom says quietly. "Austin *seems* like a nice boy. But how well do you know his family? What if the tabs offer them money to talk about you?" She waves her spoon at me. "Would they do it?"

"No." I shake my head firmly.

"I just don't think it would hurt to put this thing with Austin on the back burner and concentrate on the *Adams Project* and Carol Ingram's publicity plan," Mom declares.

"Kaitlin, what you do in your personal life is your business," Laney disagrees. "Carol can't control that." My stomach muscles begin to relax. Go, Laney!

"You don't have to date Drew," she says firmly. "You just have to make Carol look good. Her initiative is the first of its kind at Wagman and she wants it to succeed. You don't want to be the one to cross her." She shrugs. "Fly beneath the radar. Go with Drew to the events Carol wants and let me worry about the rest. I'll make sure she doesn't overstep her bounds. Besides, there are enough hot parties around here that you can take both Austin and Drew and still have enough left over to last a year."

Okay.

"I'll play along," I agree reluctantly. Mom and Dad breathe a collective sigh of relief.

"Good. Now let's change the subject." Laney finally relaxes enough to take a bite of her crab cake.

I bite my lower lip. "Does Hutch know about Carol's plans?"

"She said he approved it." Laney seems surprised herself. "Every last detail."

Humph. I hope Hutch knows what he's doing. I look down at my Sidekick and type quickly.

PRINCESSLEIA25: Sorry! Dinner @ 7.

For now at least, Drew and Carol can wait.

THURSDAY 6/14
NOTE TO SELF:

Have Nadine book weekly deep tissue massages @ Massage Therapy Center
Stunt workshop w/Drew — Sat. @ 8
Final swimsuit fitting Sat. @ 12
Highlights and eyebrow wax @ Fredric Fekkai/Sat. @ 3

**Movie Start Date: MONDAY! Call time: 5 AM.

SIX: *Day 1 and Counting*

Ever hear the expression "hurry up and wait?" That's perfect for describing a movie set.

The Untitled Hutch Adams Project is no exception, and we're only on day one of filming. My call time for hair, makeup, and wardrobe was 5 AM. It's now close to *three* and I've only filmed for an hour. Hutch is so busy shooting various angles of the same scene that he's needed me once so far. Below where I sit in the bleachers of the Santa Rosita Olympic Swim Center, a crew of about twenty-five people is bustling around the deck setting up the lighting and the micro-phones with stand-ins. (Stand-ins are paid to walk through the scene while the director and lighting team test the shot. That way the stars of the film don't have to hang around in costume getting annoyed. Great, huh?)

"Whose brilliant idea was it for the first day of shooting to be on location?" A sleepy Nadine grumbles as we sit on the blue plastic bleachers sipping green tea with Rodney (who is drinking a vanilla protein shake).

The ceiling rises almost two stories above the bleachers, which are illuminated by fluorescent lanterns hanging above the pool's dozen or so lap lanes. It feels a bit cool in the cavernous arena and I pull the white terrycloth robe covering my costume around my shoulders. I'm not sure if I'm really chilly in the red tank suit — my character's fictional high school, Park High, is emblazoned in big white letters across my chest — or if I'm just nervous about this movie. Despite Drew's touchy-feely tendencies and the last-minute addition of Sky, I was excited to work with Hutch before Laney dropped the publicity bombshell. I can't stop thinking about why Hutch would agree to Carol's strange request. What director wants the public to think his costars are hooking up? Hutch doesn't seem like the kind of guy who would welcome the presence of the paparazzi on set, but that's what is going to happen if they think Drew and I are dating. They'll start hanging around locations to catch a shot of Drew and me making out (for the cameras, of course). Why would Hutch want the added commotion?

My director is down below watching the chaos on the pool deck with a scowl on his face. Our assistant director, or A.D., Hank, is yelling at the second A.D. about today's call sheet while the cameramen, gaffer (who works with the cinematographer on mood and lighting), grips (manpower), and best boy (helps the gaffer with electric. FYI: best boys can be girls!) work around them to continue setting up the shot by the pool. They seem to be trying to move the equipment as close to the water as possible, risking getting it wet. After a few minutes of shouting among everyone, Hutch throws his hands up and dives in dressed in a Van Halen tee and swim shorts, splashing the nearest crew members. The crew instantly grows quiet.

"Hand me the camera." He wades over, shaking water out of his hair like a wet dog, snatches the plastic-covered camera from a gaping cameraman, and rests it on his shoulder. "If you can't get this simple task right, I'll test the shot myself."

"He must have first-day jitters too," I reason.

"Maybe. Or maybe he's just mental," Nadine whispers.

Across the pool, the extras that are paid to fill out the swim teams are practicing their cheers with a P.A. (production assistant). Drew is keeping a bunch of giggly blond extras entertained with grunt-worthy push-ups and jumping jacks. When the girls applaud, Drew removes his white tee to reveal his ripped chest and red Park High trunks.

Sky, however, is nowhere to be seen. She must be relaxing in her trailer. I wish I could do that, but I was too nervous to wait in mine to be called. I'd just pace up and down, trying not to throw up.

Liz says the first day of shooting a movie is nothing like the first day of school. In class, you have a week or so to ease into your new schedule and get used to your teachers. On movies, day one is just like day thirty-seven — you're shooting a scene, ready or not. I always find the first day scary. I'm worried about what Hutch will think of my performance and how I'll mesh with my costars, whom I'm supposed to have great acting chemistry with, even if we practically hate each other. And it always makes my head spin when we start shooting a scene from the middle of the script.

HOLLYWOOD SECRET NUMBER SIX: Movies don't shoot in chronological order. If your script is set in London *and* New York, you'll unreasonably increase production costs if you jet back and forth a hundred times. Instead, productions shoot all the related scenes in one city before flying to the next. The same principle goes for productions that require numerous scenes spread out over the course of a movie to be shot at the same private home in Nantucket. Usually they'll shoot all the house scenes together even though they're out of sequence.

And on the off chance a production calls for an Olympic-size pool that is booked for all of June and July except for today, they'll probably shoot there on the first day of production.

"Kaitlin, we're going to need you in five," Hank yells in to the stands. He nervously runs a hand through his short, brown spiked hair. He confided to me that he's worked on all of Hutch's projects, even if they're all beyond "stressful." Hmm. Maybe that's why Hank is so pasty white and thin.

Stressful. Now that I've signed on to work with Hutch, everyone I meet tells me how brilliant the blockbuster genius is ... and how stressful it is to work for him. Why couldn't anyone have warned me *before* I signed on?

"No problem!" I yell back cheerfully. I remove my robe,

hand Nadine my tea, and begin walking down the bleacher steps. That's when I see Liz. She's wearing jeans and a Strokes concert tee underneath. Liz is weaving in and out of the crowd, sidestepping the craft services cart that's rolling towards her and ducking under a grip holding a large handle with a light.

"Look who's finally here," Nadine mumbles under her breath. My "talk" with Nadine didn't go so well. She didn't seem convinced that having Liz around would free her up and now I'm regretting offering Liz the job. It's too late now though.

"Sorry," Liz pants. "I missed the bus that would take me here and had to wait for the next one."

"She missed the bus," I hear Nadine mutter.

"I don't know how people deal with public transportation!" Liz continues anxiously as she watches Nadine. "Anyway, when I got to security they said my name wasn't on the list. I tried calling Nadine, but she didn't answer her cell."

I look at Nadine. She pulls her cell from her back pocket and checks the screen. "No service," she says, looking surprised. "I'm sorry, Liz. I told them your name at the door."

"I knew you weren't thrilled about me being here, but I couldn't believe you would ban me from the set!" Liz jokes.

I laugh nervously. I told Liz not to say anything about what I told her.

Nadine's face is bright red. "It's not that I don't want you here, it's just that I have a routine and I don't like it being messed with."

"When school is out and I'm here full time, I promise I'll stay out of your way," Liz offers quickly, holding her hands up in peace. "I'll do whatever you ask me, no questions asked. You're the boss."

"Okay." Nadine looks relieved. "I'm sure I have a few things that I could use help with."

Crisis averted.

"Couldn't find anything better to do than tag K around this summer?" I hear a familiar voice say.

GROAN. If only bliss could have lasted longer than five seconds. . . .

"Hi, Sky," Nadine yawns.

Liz turns around smugly, ready with a witty comeback I'm sure, but jumps backwards when she sees Sky. "What happened to your hair?" Liz asks in horror.

Sky looks rattled. She tightens the candy apple red robe around her chest. "I dyed it blond," she says defensively, smoothing her slicked hair, which has been groomed to look as if she's swum in the pool, like mine. "It's for my character. Madison, hand me a mirror," she barks to her assistant.

Madison quickly produces one from the oversized black canvas bag hung over her shoulder. "Hi, Nadine, Kaitlin, how are y'all?" She's dressed too formally for a movie shoot. Everyone here is in beat-up jeans, old t-shirts, and sneakers, but Madison is in crisp white linen pants and a navy silk sailor-style top. I guess Sky didn't tell her what to expect.

Madison turns to Liz and extends her hand, which I notice is trembling. "I'm Madison. And you are?"

Liz smiles. "I'm Kaitlin's second assistant," she says coolly, looking directly at Sky.

"Oooh!" Madison squeals. "How nice. I'm new too! Are ya from around here? I'm from the great state of Louisiana. We don't have half as many Starbucks as y'all have here. Who needs to drink that much coffee?"

"Second assistant?" Sky interrupts. She drops the black mirror and it shatters. Madison dives on the ground to retrieve it. "How come I don't have a second assistant?"

"I guess they didn't think you needed one." Liz walks down a step so that she's eye to eye with Sky, who runs a hand through her wet hair and tightens the sash around her robe, preparing for a screaming match. "I mean, it's not like you're the *lead*," Liz points out nonchalantly.

"Girls, we're ready for you," the second A.D. calls.

"What's her name again?" Sky whispers quickly to Madison. Madison fumbles for a yellow spiral notebook tucked in the pocket of her dark denim jeans.

"Tracy. Likes smoothies and spa pedicures," Madison whispers.

"We'll be right down, Tracy!" Sky yells exuberantly, smiling in Hutch's direction even though he's busy yelling at Daniella from the pool.

I roll my eyes at Nadine and Liz, hand them my robe, and follow Sky down the stairs. As I leave, I hear Madison say,

"Do you girls know how to make a schedule? Sky said I should look at Kaitlin's bible for ideas. Isn't writing in the Bible sacrilegious?" I turn and see Nadine put her face in her hands.

Sky and I walk over to where Hutch is standing shoulder-high in the cloudy chlorine-heavy water. "Come on, come on!" he yells. "Time is money."

Several of the extras I saw earlier are already gathered. We're all in matching red or blue tanksuits, to mark the rival swim teams, and have swim caps or goggles wrapped around our heads. The guys are dressed in baggy swim trunks. Drew pushes through the group and takes a spot next to me.

"Looking good, Katie Bear." I notice him checking out my butt and I glare at him.

"You know what this scene is about," Hutch says to our group after we've rehearsed it once. He turns to Sky, Drew, and me. "The three of you are competing in the 800 race for the school. It's an endurance race, and Regina will be the starter, followed by Piper," Hutch says, motioning to the slim freckled redhead standing next to me.

"When Piper appears to be drowning, Carly and Dono-van will dive in to save her, while Regina hangs back and watches from the other side of the pool. As the two of you pull her out, your teacher, Mrs. Murphy, will yell at you both for messing up the race. Got it?" We all nod. "Kaitlin, I'll be looking for a huge range of emotion on your face as I pull in for the close-up shot. You're confused, bewildered, unsure of what's happening." I nod, aware that all eyes are on me now. "Okay, we're going to try to do this whole scene seamlessly once through and then shoot the other angles. Everyone be on your game."

No first scene rah-rah pep talk before shooting?

"Quiet on the set!" Hank announces through a megaphone. "Extras, wait to cheer until you receive the sign." Several of the lights set up for the shot pop on and I'm so blinded I can barely make out Nadine and Liz. They are still talking to Madison. I see Liz point to me and the three of them smile.

Hank slides in front of Sky and me holding the famous black-and-white clapper. This one has an electronic time-code that will help Hutch locate specific frames during the post-production process. I hear Sky let out a long, deep breath. My heart is pounding so loud I barely hear Hank say, "*Untitled Hutch Adams Project*, scene sixteen, take one." He snaps the board shut, the sound echoing throughout the arena.

"And, action!" Hutch yells.

On cue, the crowd behind us cheers as our swim team rallies behind Sky and me, just like we practiced. Sky dives in the pool beautifully and begins racing across the lap lane against a lanky brunette from the blue team. When it's the girl playing Piper's turn to dive in, Hutch screams "cut!"

"Laura, what kind of dive was that?" Geez. Hutch doesn't have to shout. We're all nervous. Laura pulls herself up from the pool and shakes her head. We do the shot several times, each time Hutch screaming (actually screaming!) about some technique one of us has failed to master. Drew flaps his legs like a fish when he swims, Laura can't dive properly, and my freestyle doesn't look convincing. Sky, it seems, is the only one not reprimanded. We do the race shot again and again, for almost an hour, before Hutch is finally content.

"Took you guys long enough, but you finally got it," Hutch concedes gruffly. "Catch your breath while we set up the next shot. Kaitlin, Drew, Sky, and Paula." Hutch points to the actress playing Mrs. Murphy. "Stay close by. I don't want to have to look for you when I need you." I rub my sore wet arms and walk to the edge of bleachers.

Nadine hurries down the steps and throws my robe around me. It feels good to get warm. Rodney hands me a cup of tea. Madison watches all of us intently and then jumps up to do the same for Sky.

"Kates, the reason you're having trouble with your strokes is because you're not breathing right," I think Rodney mumbles. It's hard to tell when he's talking with his mouth full. He takes another spoonful of the vanilla ice cream he got from the craft services table and continues. "You should turn your head to breathe every four strokes, not two. I can't believe someone didn't correct you." I watch Rodney make the arm motion and pretend to turn his head to breathe. I know he's right, but it's hard not to laugh.

"Is this your trainer, Kaitlin?" Our producer Daniella asks as she walks in on Rodney making a fish mouth. Daniella's small frame looks even tinier than usual in tight jeans and a green long-sleeved tee.

"No, my bodyguard," I say, and introduce them both.

"Her bodyguard slash chauffeur, but I'm also training to be a stuntman," Rodney says proudly. I notice he's discreetly placed the cup of ice cream on the bleachers behind him.

"Really?" Daniella seems genuinely interested. "Where did you study?" Rodney explains he trained at Action Actors Academy and Benny the Jet's Gym, both in L.A., and Daniella listens intently while I watch another scene unfold in front of me. Hutch is talking to Hank and waving his arms wildly.

"I think we can use you," I hear Daniella tell Rodney. What? "We definitely need some extra stuntmen for a few chase scenes."

"Thank you," Rodney says gratefully. "You won't be disappointed with my work."

I hug Rodney tightly. "Way to go, Rod! I'm so happy for you. You deserve this."

"Thanks, Kates." He squeezes me back.

Daniella smiles. "I'll put you in touch with our stunt coordinator. He'll get you on the schedule." The three of us hear something crash to the ground, and we jump.

"NO, NO, I don't care how much it costs! I want it this way!" Hutch booms, knocking a plastic plate full of raspberry crepes off the food cart next to him. The set is quiet. When he realizes everyone's watching, Hutch walks over to a P.A. holding the megaphone and grabs it from him.

"Everyone, we're going to take a one-hour break." Hutch's voice echoes in the swim center. "I'm not feeling at peace with this next shot. I need to think about the consequences of shooting it the way it's written before we continue. We'll call you back to the set when we're ready." Daniella purses her lips, but doesn't appear surprised as two P.A.s rush to give Hutch an orange yoga mat and a candle filled with incense. Hutch brings the mat to the edge of the pool, sits cross-legged, and as if no one is around, closes his eyes and begins to hum. Hank throws his hands up and walks away in a huff. As he passes Daniella and me, I could swear I hear him mumble, "He's nuts, you know that?"

"Nuts, but brilliant," she whispers back calmly.

"Do you guys want to get in on this?" A P.A. asks as he walks by. He's holding an upside-down baseball cap filled with tiny pieces of paper.

"What is it?" I ask as I peer into the worn blue hat.

"Hutch is offering $5,000 to the person who comes up with the title of the movie," the pimply guy says. "The winner will be announced at the wrap party." On movie shoots, it's customary for crews to do several money pools. I've gambled on baseball games, the World Cup finals, and even played "Pick the winning card from the deck and win a $1,000." Usually the stars of the movie up the pot by putting in more than the required bet. I remember Mac Murdock pledged $1,000 of his own money for the World Cup lottery we did during the *Off-Key* shoot.

"That's how he's coming up with the title?" Daniella questions. "If you'll excuse me, I have to go talk to him." She hurries across the deck only to be stopped by another P.A. guarding Hutch's meditation zone.

"Come on," Nadine says, appearing at my side again with Liz. Liz has the bag with my iPod, magazines, and script loaded in her arms. "Let's get you some dry clothes while Hutch thinks about the consequences of shooting the next scene as written." We giggle. As Nadine puts her arm around me and we begin walking away, Madison blatantly stares at me. When I catch her eye, she looks startled and breaks into a smile, revealing two crooked front teeth.

"Madison, what are you waiting for?" Sky seethes, pushing past all of us. "Get me another towel. I think one of my extensions is falling out."

"Maddy seems sweet," Liz says, watching them both. "I can't believe she's stuck with Sky for a boss."

"Better her than you," Nadine semi-jokes as she watches Madison run ahead of us.

I'm overcome by the smell of incense. Behind me, I can hear Hutch's humming get louder and louder.

Forget Madison's abuse and Hutch's first meltdown. You know what's really scary about this movie set? We're on day one.

MONDAY 6/18
NOTE TO SELF:

Tues., Wed. call times: 6 AM @ the soundstage
Tues. night — ALMA awards with Drew
Thurs. — 7 AM — sword play with Sky @ Paulo's studio
    10 AM — accent class
Thurs. call time: 3 PM — location in Malibu
DAY OFF??? Ck w/Nadine

seven: *Awkward Conversations*

"... And he made me step in it fourteen times! *Dog poop!* How many different ways can you shoot someone stepping in dog poop?" I cradle my cell phone under my chin as I peer out of the ivory plastic blinds of my trailer. It's parked on the backlot at Wagman Brothers Studios, where we're shooting on the soundstage today. I'm looking for Liz, who is on her way back from craft services with our lunch.

"That's disgusting!" Austin groans, although his laughter says otherwise.

Hearing his voice is like drinking peppermint tea from Elixir & Tonics (my favorite tea shop in L.A.) — I can literally feel my stress level dropping. We've been shooting nine days now, and I'm talking about *long* days. Last night I left the set at one AM and was due back at seven thirty. "Thankfully it was fake," I giggle. "They made it out of brown paint, cereal, and rubber cement."

"Are you serious?" Austin stops laughing. "That's pretty cool."

"Yep. Just one of the fascinating movie factoids I can tell you, Meyers. I'm saving the rest for when you visit," I joke, even though the situation is serious. I've put off telling Austin about Drew till we could talk in person, but I've only seen him once in the past two weeks when he was in the middle of his team's lacrosse finals, which they lost. Not exactly the best place for a tête-à-tête.

"Sorry." Austin suddenly sounds beat. "Between all those practices Coach Connors scheduled to get ready for the finals and having to finish my Civil War term paper, I haven't had a minute to breathe. School may be out, but the team has had to do all these newspaper interviews about Clark making it to their first-ever lacrosse finals, and then I've had lacrosse camp with the kids every day and it's just been chaos.

"You're a celebrity," I tease. "I saw the big picture of you in the *Santa Rosita Ledger*." I sent Liz out to get me a copy.

"I look ridiculous," Austin mumbles. "I don't know why they ran such a big picture of a sweaty me and such a small shot of the team. The article was about the team!"

"Welcome to my world. If you're cute, you sell newspapers." We both laugh. "I wish I could have been at the game," I add wistfully.

"Come on now, you had to work," Austin points out.

"I know." Sigh. Things are going so well between us. But I can't avoid the Drew conversation any longer. "There's something I've been meaning to talk to you about and I was trying to avoid doing it over the phone, but we've both been so busy and . . ."

"Are you okay?" I can hear the concern in his voice and my heart melts. "Is it Sky? You haven't said much about what's going on at that movie set."

I bite my lip. "I haven't wanted to burden you," I admit.

"Burden me?" Austin laughs. "That's what boyfriends are for, or didn't anyone tell you that? I think about what you're doing all the time. It would be nice to know — hint, hint — what's going on."

"Let's just say Hutch could give your Coach Connor a run for his money in the power trip department," I sigh. "But I can complain about that later. This is more important. It's about Drew." I catch Nadine look up from her spot on the couch in the living room. She's wearing her usual set en-semble of a fitted tee, jeans, and running shoes. She quickly goes back to reading e-mails on her BlackBerry.

There's a long silence. "What about him?" Austin asks finally.

"I wasn't completely upfront about why he was acting so weird at the Xbox party," I explain nervously. "The truth is . . . Drew and I went out a few times." I wince, waiting for his reaction. "It was before I even met you," I babble, trying to fill the uncomfortable silence. "I just didn't know how to tell you that I was spending the summer working with my moronic ex."

Austin groans. "So now instead of thinking of you all day, I'm going to be thinking about what you're doing with Drew."

"I can't stand the guy," I insist. "You have nothing to worry about."

"I wish you would have told me," Austin says. He sounds annoyed, but not angry. "It's not like you don't know all about my ex."

When I think of him and loathsome Lori, I want to vomit. I guess I see his point. "I promise I'll be more open," I vow, knowing that I'm still sort of lying by not telling Austin that Drew and I were actually together three months and how much he hurt me. This is why Austin can't know about Carol's crazy publicity machine either. If Austin knew how much time Drew and I are going to have to spend together, it would kill him.

"Well, now you're on girlfriend probation," Austin jokes "which means you have to do exactly what I say."

"And what's that?" I question, relieved that the Drew topic didn't blow up into a huge fight.

"You have to have dinner with my family. My mom is making my favorite dish, pot roast, to celebrate Clark making it to the finals, and she promised she'd wait till your next day off to do it."

Dinner with Austin's family? Oh God. I've never even met Austin's dad before, and my awkward conversations with his mom and sister, Hayley, have always gone something like this: "Hi! How are you? Is Austin home? Thanks!"

I realize I've left a long pause. "Dinner sounds great." I fumble for the week's schedule, which is somewhere on the narrow oak kitchen table. When I find it, I scan for my day off. "How about Friday?"

"Friday it is. FINALLY. I was beginning to forget what you looked like," he murmurs softly.

My heart melts, but the moment is interrupted by the arrival of Liz. She looks aggravated. She's carrying a tray overflowing with three raspberry smoothies, my turkey and low-fat Swiss panini, Nadine's vegetable soup, some soy cookies, and a bowl of fresh blackberries. Several of the weekly tabloids are tucked under her right arm. I jump up to help as Nadine continues to check e-mails.

"I'll be the one carrying the tiramisu," I say into the phone, referring to Austin's favorite dessert. Liz sets the smoothies noisily on the table and wordlessly holds the tabloids under Nadine's nose. "I'll call you later," I add hastily, watching the tense interaction. Liz hasn't seemed to enjoy her first full-time work week on set. Unlike shoots in the past, there's been no time to lounge around the trailer talking with me in between scenes. Nadine has kept Liz pretty busy with paperwork, food runs, and phone calls. I take a seat in the softly lit breakfast booth, grab the remote, and turn on the fifteen-inch flat-screen TV. Maybe some *SNL* reruns on Comedy Central will lighten the mood.

HOLLYWOOD SECRET NUMBER SEVEN: If you're interested in where a celebrity ranks on the Hollywood food chain, check out the size of their trailer. Mobile mansions are a star's home away from home. For the *Adams Project*, Sky, Drew, and I got Star Waggons' Megastars. The trailers are tri-leveled with a sofa bed, wardrobe closet, full-size shower, flat-screen TV, and separate living room. I like my digs, but a true A-lister like Julia or Angelina wouldn't be caught dead in this aging wagon. (They'd probably have the Star Waggons' Supreme — a forty-three-footer that is so tricked out that most studios beg stars not to even ask for one. They have a full kitchen with Corian counters, hardwood floors, a bedroom that can fit a queen-size mattress, and a forty-two-inch plasma screen with surround sound.) Smaller cast members are housed in "bangers" — two- and three-door trailers (nicknamed for the banging sound they make when the door slams shut) that usually have several separate dressing rooms. Matty was hoping for one of those. Instead he's in a Honeywagon, or as he calls it, "the slums." There are ten separate tiny dressing rooms without any amenities, not even your own bathroom. Kind of explains why he's taken to hanging out in my trailer so much.

"HEY!" Matt appears and slides into the booth next to me. He's not on the shooting schedule today so he's dressed casually in jeans and a black zip-up sweater. He eyes the sandwiches on the table. "Where's mine?" he asks no one in particular.

"Liz, can you go get Matty a sandwich?" Nadine asks as she sits down at the table and grabs her own lunch.

"You're kidding me, right?" Liz looks wild. "I thought we were *Kaitlin's* assistants! Why can't you go? I've got to meet Daniella in ten minutes to help her find an inexpensive alternate site for the dance scene."

"Me?" Nadine bristles. "You were late again this morning and now you can't even run back to craft —"

"I'm not that hungry actually," I jump in. "Matty can have half of mine." Matty grabs half the panini from my plate and digs in.

"Fine." Liz takes a seat next to Nadine, who is already flipping through the weeklies. Liz pulls her frizzy brown curls into a bun and covers them with a lilac scarf that matches the fitted tee she's paired with comfy distressed jeans.

I notice Nadine look closely at a story with a picture of me and Drew. "Tell me," I sigh as I put one napkin on my lap and tuck one into my shirt like a complete geek. I cannot stain this denim mini-dress for the next scene. Wardrobe will kill me.

Liz peers over Nadine's shoulder. "'Kaitlin Burke and costar Drew Thomas are looking pretty cozy on the set of *The Untitled Hutch Adams Project* these days, despite cries from Kaitlin's camp that she's got a steady boyfriend. "Ridiculous," was all Kaitlin's flack Laney Peters would say when asked about the allegations. "I won't dignify this trash talk with a comment." One thing Peters can't deny is the past — Burke and Thomas dated last year.'"

GROAN. I bury my face in my hands.

"Well, look at it this way — at least you told Austin you and Drew dated, even if you lied about how long you went out," Nadine says with a stern look.

"You finally told him?" Liz asks. I quickly fill her in on

Austin's and my conversation and how I still haven't told him about Carol's diabolical plan.

"Who cares?" Matt mumbles, munching on a soy cookie. "I don't know why you're even bothering to worry about the appearances with Drew. You can't control what's written."

"Or what they reprint from the past," Nadine adds. "You better hope those pictures of you and Drew lying on the wet sand don't resurface."

"Or quotes from that obnoxious interview Drew did with *GQ*," Liz says quietly. It wasn't bad enough Drew cheated on me, then he bragged in great detail about making out with me. The *GQ* interview was particularly painful not only because he talked about what a great chest I had, but because he said I was gullible to think he wanted a serious relationship. "She was just another conquest," I remember he told the interviewer dismissively. The memory still stings.

I slide my half of sandwich over to Matty. "I think I've lost my appetite," I groan. I grab the magazine, unable to keep from reading my story. When I'm done I scan the one next to it about Mina Burrows. Apparently she's been dating a P.A. she met on her last movie. The two of them went to Maui for a long weekend and he taught her surf. Why can't *Hollywood Nation* write sweet stories like that about me?

I push aside the magazine and I pull out my Sidekick to return some e-mails. My cell phone rings and I recognize the commander-in-chief ring tone Liz programmed.

"KAITLIN?" Laney shouts when I pick up. I can hear cars

whizzing by in the background, which means she's driving. At least she's not stuck in traffic. There are few things Laney hates more than being held hostage somewhere against her will. "CAN YOU HEAR ME?" Everyone at the table laughs.

"Yeah, Laney, we can all hear you," I answer, holding the phone away from my ear.

"GOOD," she barks. "HOLD ON, KAITLIN. I'M DOING SEVENTY! HOW MUCH QUICKER DO YOU WANT ME TO GO?" She must be yelling at another driver. I wait for her to finish. "I GOT A CALL FROM THAT WITCH CAROL THIS MORNING," Laney says, and I realize she's talking to me again.

My stomach clenches. "What did she say?"

"SHE WANTS YOU AND DREW TO GO TO THE *ANTARCTICA* PREMIERE TOGETHER ON FRIDAY NIGHT AND . . . WHAT? I DID SIGNAL!"

"Signal? Laney, who are you talking to?" I hear Laney let a few obscenities fly before the phone grows quiet. "I can't go on Friday. I'm having dinner with Austin's family. Laney? Are you there?" Liz offers me my smoothie, but I shake my head.

"I PULLED INTO STARBUCKS," Laney says suddenly. She's still yelling, even without the traffic drowning her out. "I NEED CAFFEINE. TALKING TO CAROL GAVE ME A HEADACHE."

Nadine points to her watch. Could it really be after one already? I have to get back to set. We're shooting in the futuristic high school set they constructed on soundstage eight. We were supposed to start shooting there yesterday, but we were delayed because Hutch felt our set gave off bad vibes. He called in a Feng Shui expert to analyze the space. "Laney, I have to be back to set in ten," I explain. "What am I going to do about Friday?" I rub my temples soothingly.

"Kaitlin," Laney says in a warning tone that resembles my mom. "We talked about this. You have to do appearances. Carol's office didn't *ask* that you go, they demanded. And you know I usually don't take demands from anyone. *Antarctica* is a Wagman Brothers film and Hutch is an executive producer on it. He's going to be there."

"I'll do both," I say resolutely. "The premiere probably isn't till eight anyway."

"You've got it. I told Carol you'd have to meet Drew there because you have an interview beforehand." Laney snickers. "You don't, but at least this way it doesn't look like the two of you actually showed up together."

YES. Round one goes to us! Laney says she'll fax the details to Nadine. As we're hanging up, I hear my trailer door open and see Madison. She's dressing down like the rest of the crew now in ripped jeans and a tight pale blue zip-up hoodie.

"Sorry to bother y'all, but I wanted to tell ya that filming has been pushed back to 1:30," Madison says sweetly.

"Thanks, Maddy," Liz says, getting up. "Are you free for coffee later? I have a meeting with Daniella, but I could hook up with you at the production office at three. We can pick up tomorrow's callsheets." Madison nods. Wow, I didn't know they got so chummy.

"Make sure you drop off Kaitlin's boots to wardrobe before you go," Nadine warns. "They chewed *me* out when *you* forgot to return the jacket from yesterday's scene after you left early to get a pedicure." Liz rolls her eyes at Madison as they head out.

With the extra fifteen minutes, I answer a few more e-mails and finish my smoothie. I'm not going to eat again till we wrap around seven so I better put something in my stomach. As I open the door to leave I almost get barreled over by Hank. Sweat is dripping down his face and he's out of breath. "You're ten minutes late!" he huffs.

I feel my body go numb. "What are you talking about? Madison said we were delayed fifteen minutes."

"I told her we were starting fifteen minutes *early*! She must have gotten it backwards," Hank groans. He holds his head. "Hutch is throwing a fit. You better get down there." He grabs my arm before Nadine can utter a word and the two of us run full-out across the backlot to soundstage eight. As we race through the crowded set, I hear Hutch.

"An hour lunch isn't long enough, Kaitlin?" Hutch bellows as the P.A.s look on worriedly. Sky, Drew, and a dozen or so extras are already on their marks in the round room constructed to resemble our science lab.

"I'm so sorry, Hutch." My cheeks are burning hotter than the lights filling the crowded room. There must be about twenty-five people witnessing my embarrassment.

"I expect more from my lead, Kaitlin," Hutch says simply. I walk across the quiet set to my egg-shaped seat next to Sky.

What is she smiling about? Wait a minute. Did Madison accidentally mess up the call time or did she do it on purpose?

"Are you guys ready?" Hutch asks as he stares at me with his trademark scowl.

"As always, Hutchie," Sky cheers. "Finally ready, K?"

"Ready." I push the betrayal out of my mind for the moment.

TUESDAY 6/26
NOTE TO SELF:

Dinner w/ A's family — Fri. @ 5:00
**Ask Nadine or Liz to pick up tiramisu!!!
—Find dress 4 *Antarctica* premiere
—What time is premiere?? Limo pickup from A's @ 8??
—Remind N & L 2 double-check ALL calltimes!

eIGHT: *Dinner at Austin's*

So this is what a family dinner feels like.

It's not takeout from Chow Mein's eaten out of the styro-foam containers or Matty and me dining on whatever left-overs the housekeeper serves us while Mom and Dad dash off to another benefit at the Travoltas'. At Austin's, a family dinner is the whole family eating something they actually cooked themselves.

"More tea, Kaitlin dear?" Austin's mom pours the steam-ing water over my chamomile tea bag into a dainty floral cup.

"Do you want another cookie, Kaitlin?" Hayley, Austin's eleven-year-old sister, practically knocks Austin off his chair as she leans over him to offer me the plate piled high with chocolate chip cookies. "I baked them myself."

"Funny, no one's offered me more dessert." Austin winks at me. He looks adorable in a blue-and-white striped oxford and khakis. His usually messy hair is styled with gel and he smelled like Reeses Peanut Butter Cups when he kissed me hello in the doorway. "Stop fawning over Kaitlin, you guys. You're making her uncomfortable!"

Mrs. Meyers and Hayley both turn as red as the faux-finished crimson walls. Their dining room has a warm country vibe: the oval dining table and buffet are distressed black, there's Americana placemats and napkins, and the wrought-iron light fixture hanging above our heads has roosters on every shade.

"Sorry, sweetie." Mrs. Meyers looks from me to Austin.

I knew my first dinner with Austin's family would be awkward. I thought they wouldn't want anything to do with me after the Rachel stunt, but Hayley, who talks a mile a minute even with a mouth full of metal, says she and her mom actually felt sorry for me. ("I can't believe you had to pretend to be someone else in order to get a few weeks of R&R!") It doesn't hurt that both of them are huge fans of *FA*. Mr. Meyers, on the other hand, hates all TV shows except *Law and Order*. ("The early years, not this new stuff," he grunted.) Hayley was mortified, but I think it's cool he's never seen an episode of *FA*. To be honest, I haven't seen that many of them myself.

HOLLYWOOD SECRET NUMBER EIGHT: Many stars don't watch their own work. Yes, stars are egotistical, but you'd be surprised at how many of us are uncomfortable watching our celluloid selves. At movie premieres, some stars actually do the red carpet and then slip out when the lights go down. Sometimes they have legitimate reasons and can't stay, but the reason could also be they don't want to sit through the movie again. If you're scheduled to do a world publicity tour for the film, you don't want to see it in Los Angeles and then again in London, Munich, and Tokyo. (Personally, I find it hard not to laugh at myself dubbed over in Japanese with a too-high baby-girl voice.) As for TV, many of my costars don't watch *FA*. It's nothing personal. It's just that we spend so much time filming it, and so many hours on set, who has the time — or desire — to watch all those episodes?

"I'm fine," I squeak. I'm the one who should feel uncomfortable tonight! Mrs. Meyers had to keep the pot roast warm after I got stuck on set. I was supposed to be off today, but Hutch rewrote another scene and I had to work. Then I forgot the tiramisu Nadine ordered from Sweet Tooth and she had to *deliver it* in the middle of dinner. I'm still embarrassed. I'm sure I'm going to fail the girlfriend litmus test.

"This tiramisu is delicious, Kaitlin!" Mrs. Meyers says, taking another serving. Mrs. Meyers told me she eats what she wants, stays slim, and never works out. Mom would be super jealous. "You'll have to give me directions to that bakery," she adds.

"Of course." I shove a spoonful of the rich dessert into my mouth, happy to be talking about something other than myself. "Austin and I went there a few weeks ago and he liked it so much I had to get it for tonight." I reach for Austin's hand under the table. He rubs my hand softly and I get woozy.

"Isn't it good, Jack?" Mrs. Meyers prods her husband.

Mr. Meyers looks up from his *L.A. Times* and removes his black wire-rimmed glasses. Austin had warned me that his dad reads the paper during dessert. Hey, at least he sits at the table.

"What? Yes, great," he responds absentmindedly. Hayley looks just like him. They both have dark brown hair and are giants. The only trait Hayley shares with Austin are those magnetic turquoise eyes. God, do I love those eyes.

"Austin, remember those Neiman Marcus cookies Lori used to bring?" Mr. Meyers asks, referring to Austin's ex who hated me. "Did you ever get the secret recipe? I loved those."

Now it's my turn to blush. Lori could cook? I knew she was popular, beautiful, and sporty, like Austin's own family (Austin's dad rushes from his day shift with the L.A. police department to Hayley's school, where he coaches her soccer team!), but she could cook too?

"DAD!" Hayley scolds.

Mrs. Meyers purses her lips. "Really, Jack," she whispers.

"What?" Mr. Meyers looks at Austin and me with such a confused look that I want to laugh. "What did I say?"

"Um, no, Dad, never got the recipe." Austin coughs. "They weren't *that* good."

"Maybe you're right," he says innocently. "It was the blondies she made that I loved." Now I can't help but giggle.

"So where are you going tonight, Kaitlin?" Hayley asks quickly. She leans her bare elbows on the table and puts her hands under her chin, ready for a full explanation. She could listen to Hollywood fodder all night.

"It's a premiere for *Antarctica*, the new movie with Murray Scott," I explain to everyone as Mr. Meyers returns to the business section. "I wish I could stay, but this movie was made by the studio putting out my Hutch Adams film, so I have to support it." I look at Austin apologetically. We had originally talked about starting our long overdue *Star Wars* marathon tonight.

"Why aren't you going, Austin?" Hayley asks.

"They only gave Kaitlin one ticket," he explains nonchalantly. "No biggie. Who wants to stare at Murray Scott's mug for two hours?" I think Austin was disappointed, but how was I going to explain why Drew was meeting me there?

"Murray Scott is so hot." Hayley counters. While the two of them argue, I peek at my watch: 7:15. I have to get changed before Rodney picks me up. I quickly excuse myself from the table and run up to Austin's room, where my dress is hanging in the garment bag Nadine brought along with the tiramisu. I unzip it and look inside. She's sent my new black LAMB slip dress. Black sequins cover the peek-a-boo bodice, which cuts off at my knees and is replaced by an inch of black feathers. Very 20s. After I dress and give my face a quick swipe of lipstick and mascara — I refused Laney's offer for Paul and Shelly to help me get ready at Austin's — I begin to walk down the stairs gingerly in my strappy stilettos. I'm on the second step when I hear the doorbell ring.

"I'll get it!" Hayley yells as she races from the dining room to the front door. She whips the screen door open. "Drew Thomas!" she practically chokes.

DREW???

"Hey, cutie," Drew steps into the doorway wearing a black suit, black shirt, and no tie. His dark hair looks wind-blown.

"You're not Rodney!" I say accusingly. It was the first thing that came to mind.

Drew's smile turns to confusion as Austin appears. "No, he's meeting us there." Drew stares at his competition. "Carol told me to pick you up here."

"Carol? How did Carol know where I was?" I can hear myself growing hysterical.

Drew looks at me oddly. "Madison told her."

"WHAT?" Wait a minute. How did Madison get her hands on my schedule? I can only imagine how bad this must look to Austin's family. I'm being picked up at his house by *another guy*. Wait till I get my hands on Madison. And Sky. Sky is definitely behind this and I'm going to finally kill her.

"Can I have your autograph?" Hayley asks eagerly.

"Do you have a pen and paper, sweetie?" Drew asks.

"Nope. We're all out." Austin glares at Drew and just then Mr. and Mrs. Meyers appear in the doorway.

"Oh more company," Mrs. Meyers says in surprise.

"Have another date, Kaitlin?" Mr. Meyers asks with not a hint of jokiness in his voice. Gulp.

"I need ten minutes," I tell Drew, shoving him backwards out the door. "I'll meet you in the car."

"But we're going to be late," I hear him protest as I slam the front door shut behind me. I turn around and face the mob.

"Drew is not supposed to be here," I explain quickly. "Rodney, that's my driver," I tell the Meyers, "was supposed to pick me up."

"To meet Drew?" Austin interrupts. "I thought you were going solo."

"Uh, Hayley, let's give your brother a moment," Mrs. Meyers says hurriedly and steers her daughter and Mr. Meyers away. Mr. Meyers looks back at me skeptically.

"No, they insisted the two of us go together since we're the stars of Hutch's new movie," I blurt out. "I didn't want you to get upset. It's not like I want to go with him. It's just work." Outside, I hear the horn honk. What the . . . ? Rodney wouldn't honk at me. UGH! But Drew would.

"Your date is waiting." Austin opens the door.

Someone lays on the horn again and holds it. I have to go. Carol will freak if we're late for the red carpet. "I'll call you later," I whisper. "Thanks for dinner, Mrs. Meyers," I yell back into the house.

"You're welcome, Kaitlin," I hear her say. I'm not sure how to interpret her tone.

I lean over to give Austin a kiss goodbye and he offers me his cheek. I fight the urge to cry. I don't know what to say in thirty seconds that can change the awkward end to the evening. I turn carefully around in my three-inch heels and teeter down Austin's front steps.

nine: *The* Antarctica *Premiere*

When I reach the bottom of Austin's steps, I notice the car idling at the curb. It's an Escalade instead of a Lincoln. That's definitely not my ride! I open the back door and prepare for a fight.

"It wasn't me honking, Ms. Burke," the gray-haired driver says, nervously looking at Drew.

"What the hell is going on?" I ask the two of them angrily. "Where's Rodney?"

"Hi, Kaitlin." I hear a voice say. "This is Ashley, Carol's assistant."

"Hi, Ash." Drew grins. He points to the car phone.

"Sorry for the change of plans, Kaitlin," Ashley says, though she doesn't sound apologetic. "Carol felt it would be better if you and Drew arrived together. Madison graciously told us where to find you."

"Did anyone alert my team?" I ask tartly. "My bodyguard Rodney was supposed to meet me here. He attends all my events."

"Someone will be meeting him at your pickup location shortly to let him know about the switch," Ashley reports. "He'll meet you at the premiere."

Carol tricked us! Laney is going to FLIP OUT. I break out my Sidekick and begin to type as Ashley continues to talk.

"Make sure you pose for a lot of pictures and talk about what a great experience filming with Hutch has been," Ashley is saying. "The premiere party will be at the club LAX. We'd like the two of you to go together and take photos with Hutch. Any questions?"

"Nope," Drew answers for us both. I bite my lip to keep from screaming.

"Great. Then I have some good news Carol wanted me to share," Ashley says as the driver cruises towards West Hollywood. "The two of you have been asked to cohost the Teen Titan Awards."

"Get out? Are you serious?" Drew hollers. "That's awesome!"

Even though I'm enraged, I stop pounding out a text message to Laney and look up. I have to admit, that *is* pretty cool. I've never hosted an awards show before and the Teen Titan Awards are one of the most fun. Voting is done by real teens. I love their trophies: a beefy bronzed god or goddess holding a dumbbell.

Austin would have a blast at the Teen Titan Awards. But I guess he has to be speaking to me for me to ask him to be my date.

"Your publicists will fill you in tomorrow when they get

details from Carol," Ashley says. "Have a good night." We hear a dial tone.

"Did I tell you we'd do great things together or what?" Drew says excitedly. He slides closer. "People love our chemistry! Why else would they ask us to cohost the Teen Titan Awards?" Before I can answer, my phone rings on cue.

"WHERE ARE YOU? RODNEY IS IN FRONT OF AUSTIN'S HOUSE WAITING FOR YOU AND YOUR BOYFRIEND SAID YOU LEFT ALREADY!" I fill Laney in.

"THAT LYING SON OF A . . ." Whoa. "I SHOULD HAVE KNOWN SHE WOULD PULL SOMETHING LIKE THIS WHEN I SAID YOU WERE ONLY GOING IF YOU AR-RIVED SOLO!"

I feel nauseous.

"I bet they didn't even call Nadine!" Laney is saying. "What I want to know is how Sky's assistant got ahold of your schedule."

"You and me both," I wonder aloud.

"I've got to get to the bottom of this." I hear a dial tone.

"Did you know no one called my publicist and told her you were picking me up?" I ask Drew accusingly.

Drew shakes his head. He actually looks honest for a change, though he's so slippery it's hard to be sure. "You're with me now. They should be thrilled. The studio is."

"I don't care what the studio thinks," I snap, getting more agitated by the minute. Austin looked so upset and I can't even call him with Drew here.

"I get it. You're mad because I caused a fight with Arnold," he says. "What are you doing with that guy anyway? Sky told me he's in *high school*." Drew shudders. "You need someone who understands our lives. Arnold can't." He moves a hand onto my bare knee.

"HIS NAME IS AUSTIN!" I yell so loud the driver slams on the brakes. Thankfully we're in front of the theater. "Let's get this over with," I say, opening the door myself. The flash of lights is blinding, but I drag Drew away from the waiting paparazzi over to the press line. With a smile on my face the entire time, I answer every question they ask and try to keep Drew on track. ("Come on, Kates," Drew said in front of one reporter. "You can admit it. It's great to be together again." I quietly stepped on Drew's foot, digging my stiletto into his toes, and said, "It is onscreen.")

But once the press line is over and Drew and I are sitting in the packed-to-capacity theater's velvet-lined seats, I can't concentrate on anything but Austin. It's too risky to call him now and have a reporter overhear me sobbing my apologies into the phone, and I can't dis Hutch, who is sitting behind us, by getting up and leaving. So I sit there in silence, paying no attention to the heart-pounding thriller on screen — though the dramatic music does match my mood. I just want to go home.

"That movie was awesome," Drew says two hours later as we're dropped off at LAX, where *Antarctica* is having its premiere party. "And it didn't have a tenth of the special effects we do. Our film is going to rock." Drew attempts to take my hand as we get out of the car, and I slap it away for about the nine hundredth time tonight.

"And wait till the sequel!" he adds, ignoring my foul mood. "We're going to pull in such big bucks they'll have to pay us triple to do the next one."

I don't have a clue what *Antarctica* was like, since I was thinking about Austin the entire time, but still, I wish I had his confidence. Constant rewrites, fighting on set, reports about the rising budget cost in *EW*... it's not looking good.

Drew flashes me the thousand-watt smile that makes fans faint. "Don't worry, Katie Bear. I wouldn't sign on without you. I could always cool my heels on *Family Affair* till the next movie. You guys need some new blood on that show. You're getting stale."

"NAME," a beefy bouncer in a skintight black tee barks as we approach the doors to the club.

"Drew Thomas and Kaitlin Burke," Drew announces importantly.

The bouncer scans the long list attached to his clipboard, then looks up at me and squints menacingly. "You're in. She's not," he says gruffly. "Her name is not on here."

"That's impossible," Drew sputters as he waves over a nearby flack from Wagman. "Don't you know who she is? She's Kaitlin Burke! The star of *Family Affair*. My costar in Hutch Adams's new movie."

"Isn't Sky Mackenzie the star of *Family Affair*?" The bald

bouncer asks with a slick smile, and that's when I notice his gold front tooth.

I forgot where we were! LAX is Sky's turf since her pal DJ Arachnid spins here. She must have had me banned. On any other night, I'd be pissed, but tonight Sky's doing me a favor. "No problem," I say happily, turning to leave. It's only 10:15. If I hurry, I can call Rodney (I stupidly told him to take the night off after the pickup mixup) and call Austin before he falls asleep.

A young woman from Wagman wearing a headset rushes to my side. "Kaitlin, we're SO sorry. She should be on the list. Let her in immediately," she snaps at the bouncer, flashing her Wagman VIP pass. The guy sighs and holds open the door.

A flood of lights blinds us as we walk into the airport-themed dance space. There are mirrors shaped like airplane windows, an orb-shaped jellyfish tank behind the brightly lit bar, and a metal hangar door leading to an outdoor patio.

As I take in the scene, something hits me in the head. I whirl around, but there's no one there. When I look down on the floor, I see a lone goldfish cracker. Weird. *Ping!* Another cracker smacks my forehead. It's so dark I can't see who's throwing them. Stay calm, Kaitlin. Just do one lap at the party and go home.

Drew twirls a lock of my hair around his finger as he leans his head close to mine. I turn my face away. "Stop thinking about that jerk bouncer. You're a star. Especially in my eyes," he whispers, blowing hot air in my ear. "Stop fighting it, Katie Bear, and let's get back together. I know we can work this time. I'm different now." As he strokes my hair, we both get hit by a school of flying goldfish crackers. "What the . . . ?"

"Well, don't you two look cozy," Sky says as she makes a perfectly timed entrance. She's wearing a green and white tie-dyed dress that gathers at the waist with a large silver clip. "I wonder what your little boyfriend would think if he could see you now."

"Speaking of boyfriends, where is Trevor?" I retort, raising a question I've been curious to ask for a while. I've felt a sisterly concern for hot but naïve Trevor ever since he joined *FA*. "Did you dump him already?"

"He went back to Idaho for the summer." Sky rolls her eyes. "He was homesick. I told him I don't do long distance. Trevvie was upset, but if he misses me, he can try to win me back with some expensive jewelry in the fall."

"Nice move," Drew says admiringly. I step away from both of them in disgust. That's when I see what Sky has in her hand. It's a glass bowl of Pepperidge Farm Goldfish.

"Did you throw those at me?" I ask angrily.

"I might have slipped," she says with a slithery grin. She picks up another one and aims it at my face. "Oops!"

Why does Sky have to act like a fifth grader? That's it. I pull out my cell phone and speed-dial Rodney. "Pick me up at LAX now!" I bark, and hang up, prepared to end this nonsense with Drew and Sky once and for all before I go.

"You need to back off," I say shakily to Sky. "Stop trying to make my life miserable just because *you're* miserable playing a *smaller* role than me." Sky's eyes flare. "Oh, and if your assistant messes with my schedule again, I'm going to get her fired," I warn.

But instead of being intimidated, Sky gives me a sick smile.

I whirl around to Drew.

"Let's get something clear: You and I have no chance together," I hiss. "We're costars. Nothing more. Let's do the press we have to do, shoot our scenes, and avoid each other off-camera."

"Katie Bear," Drew coos, reaching for my arm. "Don't fight this." *Ping.* Another goldfish whizzes past my nose. I push Drew away.

"LEAVE ME ALONE! I DON'T WANT ANYTHING TO DO WITH EITHER OF YOU LYING SCHEMERS WHEN WE'RE NOT WORKING!" I snap. My chest rises and falls rapidly and it takes me a second to realize the music's stopped and half a dozen people nearby have heard me yell. A flashbulb goes off in my face, which is definitely bright red. Oh God. What have I done?

"If that's the way you want it, fine," Drew whispers, looking mortified. If there's one thing Drew can't stand, it's bad press. "You don't know what a mistake you just made," he adds, eying the crowd, which is lit up by repeated flashes.

HOLLYWOOD SECRET NUMBER NINE: If you want a successful working relationship with your ex, don't do what I just did.

Sure, making out with an ex-flame onscreen is awkward, but if it's in your job description, you've got to do it gracefully and with as few flare-ups as possible. Don't push the writers to rework your scenes together — that could cause one of you to get axed. The proper way to work with an ex is simple: keep your mouth shut, talk to each other only during takes, avoid each other off-screen. If that doesn't keep you calm, just think about the hefty paycheck you'll collect when all this is over.

Even if you're not axed, your ex can still make your life miserable — like I can immediately tell mine will. As my heart pounds and I take a seat at an empty table to wait for Rodney, my two enemies join forces. Across the dance floor, standing underneath a fake palm tree, I see Sky stroking Drew's arm as she whispers in his ear. He seems completely wrapped up in what she's saying because the next thing I know, Drew takes Sky by the hand, gives me one last cold look, and they exit the party together. I'm sure they're off to Sky's limo to plot their next move, which can only mean one thing for me: I'm in deep trouble.

FRIDAY 6/29
NOTE TO SELF:

Call Hayley to find out perfect "I'm sorry" gift for A.
Call Laney again — warn her about public freak-out. Do damage control.
Schedule extra session w/Paulo to blow off steam.

THE UNTITLED HUTCH ADAMS PROJECT

SCRIPT CONTINUED:

138 EXT. GAS STATION – DAY
CAMERA PANS the scenery – heavy rainstorm, abandoned gas station. Both Carly and Donovan are wet and scared.

CARLY
We've got to keep moving. Are you okay?

DONOVAN
I don't know. I really don't know. Why would those guys want to run us off the road?

CARLY
They want us dead, Don. I'm convinced it has something to do with what Mrs. Murphy caught us reading on her computer.... You didn't see the rest of that e-mail. It said our class was being groomed to take over the human race. Like Nazis! They've been lying to us.

DONOVAN
You're crazy!

CARLY

Think about it. Those shots she was giving Todd. He threw that desk like the Hulk on speed! They've been drugging us. Our food. Our water. The training. They're breeding us to become superhuman robots.

DONOVAN

But our parents... the school... they would never allow it.

CARLY

Unless the school was in on it. They could have given our parents some bull about how all this would help us excel. But when Mrs. Murphy's minions realized we were on to them, they decided to do away with us.

DONOVAN

Which is why they sent those guys. Do you think Regina knows? She didn't act surprised when we told her about the experiments.

CARLY

No. I've got to call her back and warn her. She's probably freaking out that we got cut off.

DONOVAN

Carly, you told Regina where we were! How else would those goons be able to show up so quickly? Regina is working for Mrs. Murphy.

Carly shakes her head defiantly, but she stops when she hears the sound of branches snapping.

CARLY
Shh.... Did you hear that? Someone's coming! RUN!

ten: *Trailer Talk*

"Nadine? Liz? Is that you guys?" I yell as my trailer door opens. The two of them had run out to do errands while I was sulking in front of the TV in full makeup and wardrobe (a bloody tee and grass-stained jeans) watching a *Gilmore Girls* rerun. I'm waiting to be called to the set to shoot a tense scene with Drew. It shouldn't be hard to act ticked off — he hasn't spoken one word to me since my blowup at LAX.

I can't tell if Drew and Sky actually like each other (if those two start dating, it's a sign of the apocalypse for sure) or are just united in their quest to destroy me. Either way, watching Drew and Sky laughing and kissing up to Hutch is unbearable. So instead of sitting on set watching the scene before mine from my comfy director's chair (yes, stars really have those), I'm hiding in my trailer, miserable and cranky. It doesn't help that Mom and Laney just blasted me over this article they had Nadine deliver. This is from the new issue of *Hollywood Nation*:

KAITLIN AND SKY — The War Rages!

Meow! As the second month of shooting begins on the set of Hutch Adams's new flick, the *Family Affair* stars are crackling more than fireworks on the fourth of July! "The bad blood is getting worse," a source tells *In the Know*. The feud between KAITLIN BURKE and SKY MACKENZIE reached a high at the *Antarctica* premiere. Kaitlin arrived with costar and former flame Drew Thomas at the premiere party at LAX and was tossed out in the cold. "LAX is Sky's turf," sniffed one pal. After Kaitlin finally got inside, things got uglier when witnesses say Sky pelted goldfish crackers at her. An onlooker tells *In the Know*, "Kaitlin lost it and began screaming. She told Drew and Sky she wants nothing to do with either of them." Drew and Sky were reportedly mortified by the public shaming and vowed to get even. "Drew wants Kaitlin, but he knows hanging out with her archenemy will make her jealous," says a set source. And since Sky broke up with *FA* costar Trevor Wainright, she's been on the prowl. "Sky thinks Drew is a great catch and can't stand seeing him waste his time on Kaitlin," adds the source. Let's hope the three of them simmer down. There's over a month of shooting left on the Adams film. Production on the new season of *Family Affair* begins in August.

For once, the tabloids didn't get it wrong.

"Carol's office is very upset!" Mom yelled when she and Laney conference-called from separate locations (Laney en route to a photo shoot with George Clooney, Mom at her Botox appointment. Shh . . .) minutes after Nadine, Liz, and I had finished reading the story. I put them on speaker phone so we could all discuss.

"CAROL IS A LUNATIC," Laney's voice screeched over the roar of the 101. "I TOLD HER I WON'T ALLOW HER TO PUT MY CLIENT IN SUCH AN UNCOMFORTABLE POSITION AGAIN," Laney said. Who knew Laney could be so supportive? I knew there was a reason why I was paying her a small fortune to rep me! "I TOLD CAROL SHE SET OFF A TICKING TIME BOMB BY SENDING DREW TO PICK YOU UP . . . WHAT? NO, YOU SLOW DOWN IF YOU DON'T LIKE MY DRIVING! GET IN ANOTHER LANE!"

"I bet Carol reminded you that she's calling the shots," Nadine replied.

"You're all missing the bigger problem," I butted in. "Madison. Sky has her trained to kill. She's messed up my call time and now she's giving out my schedule!"

"You're being too hard on her," Liz said defensively. "The pressure of being a new assistant is intense. Maddy feels terrible about screwing up."

"I talked to her about the scheduling mishap," Nadine explained. "She said Carol's office called her looking for me and when she couldn't find me, she remembered overhearing me say you were at Austin's. She found his address on MapQuest."

"That's bull!" I practically cried. "How'd she know Austin's last name, huh? I can't believe you two are defending her."

"KAITLIN," Laney yelled, honking her horn to get our attention. "THE BOTTOM LINE IS CAROL WANTS YOU AND DREW TO MAKE AMENDS. AS MUCH AS I HATE THAT CONNIVING DICTATOR, I'D HATE EVEN MORE TO SEE YOU LOSE THE TEEN TITAN AWARDS HOSTING GIG OVER THIS AND . . . AAAAHH!!!" We heard tires screeching. "THAT'S MY EXIT!"

I knew I officially lost this round, which is why I surrendered by promising to keep quiet on set. It shouldn't be hard — no one is talking to me anyway. Temporarily appeased, Laney and Mom hung up.

"Hey."

I recognize the soft voice immediately and my thoughts come crashing back down to Earth. "Austin!" I exclaim. "What are you doing here?" I throw my arms around his stiff body (he's wearing a red zip-up hoodie and navy track pants) and hold on tight.

"Uh, Liz and I have to pick up something from the production office," Nadine says hurriedly, ushering a willing Liz out the door to give Austin and me some privacy. Austin and I stare at each other, unsure of what to say.

I left Austin a message on Friday night and called him again from the Save the Sea Lions auction I had to chair on Saturday (don't ask) to talk about what happened, but he didn't want to discuss Friday's date massacre over the phone and my schedule this week has been too crazy to slip away and see him. So after a strained three-minute exchange about Austin's family ("They're fine"), peewee lacrosse ("It's work") and filming ("It's okay"), it was almost a relief to hang up. We agreed to wait until we were together to, well, duke it out.

"Camp ends at two on Thursdays so I thought we could finally talk. Is that gash real?" Austin touches the red track marks on my cheek. His fingers are warm.

"No, but it's cool, huh?" I launch into HOLLYWOOD SECRET NUMBER TEN — gory makeup tricks — avoiding what I'm sure will be an awkward conversation for just a few minutes longer. Film makeup artists are responsible for creating everything from cuts and bullet wounds to makeup looks that will age you thirty years. My set artist has been filling me in on how they do it as he applies Carly's scratches (using maroon eye shadow, a stipple sponge, a black makeup pencil, fake blood, and an ice pop stick) and gashes (tweezers, a flat wooden spatula, powder, concealer, flat cotton swabs, red bruise makeup, flesh putty, heavy black thread, and Krazy glue!). The coolest thing he's taught me is how to make fake blood. He uses Karo syrup, a splash of blue and green food coloring, and his secret ingredient — Coffeemate to control the flow of the blood gushes. I'm having fun walking around with black-and-blues instead of picture perfect makeup for a change.

"Maybe I'll hire you to do my makeup for Halloween next year." Austin gives me a slight smirk.

"Does that mean we're going to be together next Halloween?" I'm afraid to hear his answer.

Austin plops down on the tan suede couch and motions for me to sit next to him. I do, but I leave a careful few inches between us. "We'll make it that far if movie stars stop showing up at my door to take you out on dates," he semi-jokes. "I'm not used to a fight with my girlfriend making *E! News.*"

I wince. He's got a beyond-valid point. At that moment, I have an overwhelming urge to spill my guts about everything, Carol's scheme and how bad Drew hurt me, but —

What's the point in confiding in him if I lose him ... I could never forgive myself if that happened. No, I can't overload him with my stupid Hollywood problems. It's not like I'm Spider-Man and I'm saving a city.

"The head of marketing, Carol Ingram, wants Drew and me to do a ton of pre-movie release publicity together," I tell him, shoving aside the nagging feeling that telling a partial truth isn't the same as being honest. I fill Austin in on what Laney and Mom think, but leave out how she knows Carol is pushing for me and Drew to look like a couple. "I know I wasn't upfront about my history with Drew in the beginning, so when I found out I had to go to all these events with him, I didn't know how to tell you," I explain apologetically as Austin listens intently, hands resting motionless on my knees. "I knew I had to do press with Drew at the premiere, but I didn't know he was going to ambush me at your house. I SWEAR." My mouth feels like sandpaper as I wait for his reaction.

"I can *sort of* understand why you thought you couldn't

tell me about Drew," he says slowly. "But why wouldn't you tell me about this marketing woman? It sounds like she's being unreasonable."

"Dealing with crazy people is in chapter two of the celebrity handbook," I reply. Austin hasn't stormed out, which has to be a good sign. "Besides, Laney and my mom can handle Carol."

"Didn't you just say they went along with everything Carol asked for?" Austin asks, confused. "How is that handling her?"

"I don't have a choice here," I argue. "This is my job, and part of my job is doing publicity."

Austin shrugs. "I guess I thought you were hired to act. Not be a mouthpiece."

"What's that supposed to mean?" I jump up from the couch in a huff and stub my toe on the distressed black wood coffee table.

"If you didn't want to go places with Drew, you wouldn't do it," Austin says calmly. "When Coach told me I couldn't leave a four-hour practice early to make my grandfather's birthday dinner, I left anyway. I didn't care if he benched me for the finals. He didn't, but the point is he can't control my whole life."

"You don't get it," I complain. I feel the weight of everything that's happened these past few weeks crushing me at once — how Hutch is nothing I dreamed he'd be, how the stunt work has been so grueling, how Sky and Drew are beating me down. "This isn't lacrosse, Austin. This is Hollywood, and Hollywood is harsh. I don't always get a choice in what I do." Embarrassingly, I'm on the edge of tears.

Austin stands up. "Are you saying what I do isn't as important as what you do?" He doesn't raise his voice, but he sounds angry now too.

"That's—that's not what I meant," I stutter, holding up my hands in peace.

"*You're* the star, Kaitlin." Austin rests his hands on my shoulders. "The studio should be kissing your butt, not the other way around. You shouldn't let anyone dictate your career, your publicity, or your days off. Not the studio, not Laney, not your mom. Do you think someone like Mina Burrows would be bullied? No way."

How could Austin know what Mina would do? "Mina would do whatever it takes to stay on top," I say hotly. "And her boyfriend, who isn't an actor, I might add, would understand because he *trusts* her."

There's a light rap on the door and Nadine pokes her head in. I think she heard us yelling. "I hate to interrupt, but they're ready for you on set."

"Give us a second," I snap. My hands are trembling. Nadine nods and shuts the door quietly. "Can we finish this later?" I suggest wearily. I think our current conversation is only making things worse. How did things get so out of control? This sort of thing would never happen to Spider-Man.

"I guess we have to." He doesn't look me in the eye.

"Do you want to wait here or watch me film?" I ask, trying not to cry.

"I'll watch you work." Austin seems stiff.

We meet Nadine outside and the three of us take a golf cart over to the soundstage. Austin and I don't speak. Instead he talks to Nadine, who plays tour guide by pointing out where different TV shows film and what stars shoot hoops at the backlot court on their lunch hour. When we pull up to our soundstage, which is set up to look like an abandoned gas station, I show Austin to my chair, which is parked in front of a series of monitors set up to view shooting. Since the filming area is too tight for Austin to stand near, one of the P.A.s offers Austin a pair of headphones so he can listen in to Hutch's commands and our dialogue. It dawns on me that I should tell him about the scene I'm about to shoot.

"Drew and I are on the run from goons from the superhuman army," I whisper, since Hank is already issuing orders.

Austin nods, but he's focused elsewhere. I turn and see Drew and Sky staring at us.

"Is this scene okay for me to watch?" Austin asks, eyes on the ground. "I don't think I'm in the mood to see you two kiss."

"It's a fight scene," I reply curtly.

"Then you should have no problem acting mad." Austin turns to Nadine, who has just put on a pair of headphones to listen in herself, and I'm left staring at his broad back.

I'm shaking as I take my mark next to Drew. Like he has the last few days, Drew refuses to acknowledge me before Hutch calls action.

We start the scene fine. I'm so riled up, I have no problem yelling my head off, or shaking Drew — or should I say Donovan — silly while trying to prove Carly's point. But then, out of nowhere, as our characters are supposed to run for their lives, Drew kisses me passionately on the lips!

One second...two...three...four...WHEN IS HUTCH GOING TO CALL CUT? I want to scream as Drew continues to press his lips and whole body into mine. His mouth is hot and I feel like I'm suffocating. Finally, I can't stand it anymore. I push him off me and slap him across the face.

"There's bigger things at stake here than your hormones, Don!" I manage to blurt out in character.

"CUT!" Hutch yells.

Drew looks at me smugly. "I forgot how soft your lips were." He wipes his mouth with the back of his hand.

I want to slap him again so I can wipe that sly smile off his face. "You've got some nerve . . . ," I say before Hutch cuts me off.

"What was that?" Hutch asks Drew.

"It felt right, Hutchie," Drew says. "In the middle of hell, Donovan can think of nothing more comforting than kissing the girl he loves."

A few seconds of complete silence tick by as Hutch considers the suggestion. "I like it!" he finally exclaims. "Good improv."

Hutch really is crazy. "That's the stupidest idea I've ever heard," I argue, my words practically tripping over one another. I'm unable to contain my emotions. "Carly and Don are about to be captured and instead of running like lightning he stops to make out? That would never happen."

Hutch's smile turns into a scowl. Uh-oh. He puts his arm around me and pulls me aside. "Is there a problem here, Kaitlin?" Hutch pulls on his scraggly new goatee. He looks even thinner than usual, and his Doors concert tee and ripped jeans hang off him.

"No, Hutch," I say, feeling my lungs constrict.

He shakes his head. "I'm here busting my butt to make this movie better, writing and rewriting, and you can't be part of this team and just go with the moment?" His voice is a little loud and a few people stare.

I'm flabbergasted. I've never been yelled at by a director before. Especially in front of a room full of people. I can't believe he's angry over this! "I'm sorry," I whisper. "I was just trying to give you another opinion."

"I'm not feeling your dedication, Kaitlin," Hutch says, running a hand through his long, flat hair. I spy Sky and Drew watching our exchange. They're practically drooling.

"I'm completely dedicated," I assure him, trying to defuse the situation even though I feel like screaming. "I've always meant to do what you ask. *Please* don't blow this out of proportion, I beg silently. Daniella moves closer to where we're standing. My face is burning hot and I know it's not from the strong lighting.

"Don't make me regret my decision to cast you over Sky,"

Hutch whispers when he sees Daniella. I feel like I've been slapped in the face. "Let's try the kiss again."

I take a deep breath and do the walk of shame over to my mark. Drew is waiting with a wide grin.

It requires all my self-control to get through the next few takes. During one where Drew gets a little too frisky, I bite his lip. He grabs his mouth in horror.

"What? I'm just improvising!" I hiss.

When Hutch is satisfied, I rush to my director's chair to see Austin and find it empty. Nadine shakes her head sadly. Before I can ask her what happened, our unit publicist interrupts us. Lisa is the one responsible for handling set visits and interviews during production.

"Kaitlin, this is Elena from *Fashionistas*! She's doing a set visit," Lisa says cheerfully.

SHOOT! I completely forgot I had an interview.

"Can I do the interview in twenty minutes?" I beg quietly. "There's something I need to discuss with my boyfriend. He's hanging out in my trailer."

Nadine pulls me aside. "Austin left," she murmurs. "He said he had somewhere he needed to be and said to tell you he was sorry that he couldn't wait to say goodbye." Nadine studies my face for a reaction, but I turn away. Seeing Drew kiss me was more than Austin could handle and now our fight has been kicked up a notch.

"I guess I'm free to do the interview now," I say mechanically.

"Elena is going to take the golf cart back to your trailer with you and interview you on the way," she explains.

"I hope you don't mind." Elena grabs a pen, paper, and her recorder out of her bag.

"Not at all." I muster a smile. "Glad you could make it." A golf cart rolls up to the four of us and I hop in.

"Was that your boyfriend I saw you with earlier?" Elena asks excitedly, once she's seated.

I nod. At least he *was* my boyfriend this morning. Now I'm not so sure.

Elena holds the microphone out. "How are things going between the two of you?"

I inhale deeply. "Couldn't be better," I lie.

THURSDAY 7/5
NOTE TO SELF:

Ask Nadine to find a chunk of time that I can leave set.
MUST SEE A ASAP!
7/6 — Capoeira choreography session w/Paulo, Drew and Sky :(

eleven: *Fight Club*

JAB, JAB. CROSS. UPPERCUT. I hit the leather punching bag harder and harder.

"Very good, Kaitlin!" Paulo, my Capoeira martial arts trainer, yells enthusiastically in a thick Spanish accent as he watches the blows. "Keep your elbow up as you throw the hook, like this." He guides my arm in slow-motion until it impacts with the bag. Nadine thinks Paulo looks just like Sayid from *Lost* (tall, broad, longish wavy hair, dark-skinned muscular arms), which may explain why she never misses one of my workout sessions with Paulo. "Try to envision the enemy as you make contact. GOOD!"

I pound away to the beat of the African drums CD, throwing jabs like lightning (okay, at least it feels that fast for my aching arms) as sweat drips down my face. It feels good to get out some aggression.

Things between Austin and me are really weird right now. We had a major fight we couldn't finish because I got called to set, where Drew kissed me to make Austin jealous, and before I could explain to Austin what happened, he left. I know I'd be mad if things were reversed, but strangely Austin seems fine. In fact, he hasn't even brought up the lip-lock! So I haven't either. Instead, this was Austin's explanation for his disappearance: "Sorry I had to rush out of there the other day, but I forgot I had a meeting about this charity game." WHAT? I know organizing a lacrosse scrimmage between the players and the faculty to raise money for the team to go to a lacrosse clinic before school starts, but all he could talk about is how many tickets he's sold for the game and how excited everyone is to play Coach Connors. I felt like I was in a *Twilight Zone* episode. Did Austin and I not have a fight? Did Drew not kiss me? Does Austin actually understand the pressure I'm under at work and is just letting me slide on this one? Or is Austin avoiding the conversation because he's waiting to break up with me till after his all-important charity game? My head hurts just thinking about all this. I just wish I could ask him in person. I wanted to go to his scrimmage this afternoon, but I have to work.

"Let's try kicks," Paulo enthuses. I change stances, stopping long enough to pull up my black hip-hugger terrycloth pants and adjust my fitted vintage-style college tank that says NEW YORK UNIVERSITY across the chest. I got it when I visited New York this spring. I secretly dream of taking a few years off to go to college in the Big Apple.

I can hear Sky and Drew grunting through the same motions at their own punching bags — that is, when Sky doesn't stop punching to flirt. ("Wow, Drew, you have such a strong punch!") After each comment, I see Drew eagerly look for my reaction. Drew is my other problem du jour. Does he want to get back together and thought a liplock would refresh my memory or was he really trying to tick me off?

UGH. Boys. They're like French class — no matter how much I study, I'll never be fluent in the language.

"You guys seem warmed up." Paulo rubs his hands together enthusiastically. "Let's get started."

The three of us are here at Paulo's studio to choreograph the final fight sequence. This is the scene where Donovan and Carly are making their way through an airport that the superhuman camp is using as their home base; they fight the bad guys and come face-to-face with Regina (aka Sky). It's a fight to the finish, and I'm really looking forward to performing it.

We've been working on the choreography for over a month and today we're putting on the finishing touches. Daniella said Hutch wants the sequence to be lyrical, even though it's a bloodbath, which is why we've all been studying Capoeira, a martial art combining kicks, jabs, and punches with African instruments and music. Hutch says the ceremonial dance and rhythm spoke to "the heart of his humanity." I'm more cynical about this kind of statement now that I've seen him frequently yell louder than Laney does after a scandalous story about one of her clients appears on Page Six.

"Sky, you must be tired," Drew coos as he stares at me. "Do you want a lift?" Without giving her time to answer, Drew scoops Sky up and she squeals as he carries her to the center mat. He gives me a look that's obviously meant to say "See what you're missing?" I roll my eyes.

"Who wants to practice their part first?" Paulo asks. Our fight starts with Regina and Donovan facing off, then Carly steps in to confront Regina.

"We will," Sky points at me. She looks back at Drew and the two of them chuckle.

What are they up to? "I'm game," I reply calmly.

Sky begins rewrapping her wrists and fingers with tape. She pulls her blond extensions into a ponytail and adjusts her short pink spandex bottoms and matching bra top. When she's satisfied, she moves inches from my face.

Nadine, Madison, and Liz, who have been deep in conversation up until now, see Sky and me touching noses and run from their bench against the wall to the edge of the mat. Even Rodney, who is working in a corner on his own stunt routine, stops what he's doing to watch the show.

"You've got this, Sky. She's easy," Drew coaches. "And I mean that in more ways than one."

"Watch your mouth, pretty boy," Rodney grumbles.

Sky and I glare at each other, neither of us moving a muscle. This close up, I can see her sweat-smudged black eyeliner and the tiny mole above her lip. "Maybe you should read your script more and flirt with Sky less," I retort. "Carly wins this fight, remember?"

"Yeah, but Carly gets beat up pretty badly, and that's all that matters," Sky spits as she pulls her arm back and prepares to take aim. I block her punch, grab her arm, and twist it behind her, as planned. With my free hand, I jab her in the stomach, a bit harder than called for.

"Ouf!" she moans. Then she clocks me on the side of the head.

"Use the choreography, girls!" Paulo reminds us. "This isn't a bar brawl."

HOLLYWOOD SECRET NUMBER ELEVEN: Not all movie fights are fake. Some onscreen slaps, punches, and falls are real and they hurt. *Bad*. Sure, the scene is staged down to the most minute detail so that no one gets injured. But sometimes, a slap needs to be real in order to be convincing.

On *FA*, we shoot fights in slow motion, but there was this one time last season when Sam was dating a guy who spread a nasty rumor about her going all the way with him. (Not! [Neither Sam nor I have rounded second base.]) Sam was supposed to confront him and slap him across the face. The cute actor playing the jerk, Jimmy Feeney, didn't want it to look staged so he made me promise to hit him as hard as I could. It felt weird smacking him across the face, but the dailies did look amazing. Jimmy had a huge red welt on his cheek and he was so proud.

I stick my leg out to trip Sky, but she sidesteps me and kicks me in the shins.

"Sky, move your feet to the music," Paulo adds. "Remember this isn't just a fight, it's a dance. A dance of anger."

"Tell that to K," Sky seethes. "She's the one with the pent-up frustration. She didn't want Drew . . ."

"I wouldn't go that far," Drew interrupts from the side-lines, but I'm focusing too hard to turn and glare at him.

". . . But now that he's gone, she can't handle that he wants me more than he ever did her," Sky finishes, sounding shrill.

"You can have Drew," I say, unable to keep my mouth shut. I block my face with my hands. "You're used to my left-overs."

Sky looks like she might breath fire. She hits my bent el-bows with her fist, banging my forearm into my nose. I grab her arm and give her another jab to the hip.

"Your popularity is falling, K, and you want to take it out on me," Sky pants. "You know Hutch regrets the day he hired you."

The two of us must look like tigers circling their prey. We move around and around in a circle, each of us stepping for-ward to take a hit or block or punch.

"If any star is falling, it's your own," I tell her. "You're al-ways in my shadow and it *kills* you. For once, I'd like to see you get a role on your own instead of trying to steal mine." I'm so proud of my comeback I miss her fist flying at my jaw. She connects, and the pain goes shooting up my face.

"Alright, you two, that's enough!" Paulo shouts. I catch a glimpse of Drew looking on in apparent horror. "The studio will kill me if either of you gets hurt!"

"Maybe you should give them a minute," I hear Nadine suggest as Sky and I circle each other edgily. Her face is red and glistening with sweat. I wipe my own soaked brow. "These two really need to get this out of their system."

"Are ya'll crazy?" Madison butts in. "My mama will kill me if Sky's face gets bruised!"

"Your mama?" Liz asks. "Why would she care?"

"SHUT UP, MADISON!" Sky yells.

"Ah, there's the sweet Sky we know so well!" I shoot a roundabout kick to Sky's hip.

"That goes for you too," Sky screams, throwing jabs like mad. "Why don't you just go back to that dumb high school again and leave us alone."

"HEY!" Liz yells. "Take that back!"

I stick my leg out and successfully trip her. As she falls though, she grabs my leg and pulls me down as well. Two seconds later, we're on top of each other, pulling each other's hair and scratching each other's clothes. My heart is pounding and my mind seems to have gone blank. One of Sky's blond extensions comes out in my hand. Eww. Within seconds, Paulo, Rodney, Nadine, Liz, Madison, and Drew are pulling us off each other.

"Let me at her!" Sky screams, trying to pull away from Paulo's strong hands. "I'm going to kill her!" Blood is dripping down her mouth. "I hate you! I HATE you! Do you know that?"

"I hate you MORE!" I hear myself roar. Liz tugs my arm.

"ENOUGH!" Paulo commands. His loud, clear voice startles me out of my blind rage, and I immediately go limp. What's wrong with me? I'm smarter than this. Why am I stooping to Sky's level? I begin backing away from the mat, frightened of my behavior.

"EVERYONE clear the room," Paulo continues. "NOW. Except for these two." He points at Sky and me.

"Are you sure that's a good idea?" Liz asks.

Paulo points to the door. "GO."

"See you next week, Paulo," Nadine says sweetly.

I look at Sky's and my reflection in the giant mirror on the back wall. We look like we've been mugged. Our hair is wild, our shirts torn, and scratches cover every part of our exposed bodies. Our chests rise and fall quickly.

"I don't EVER want to see a display like that again!" Paulo announces when the last person out shuts the door. "Whatever is going on with you two does *not* surface in my studio." He paces in front of us. I study the dirty rubber matted floor. "You're being paid big bucks to do this scene and that's what we're going to do. Stick to the choreography and keep to the dialogue. Do you understand?" I mumble yes while Sky stares wide-eyed at her bruised reflection in the mirror. Paulo drops his face into her line of vision and repeats himself. "I said, 'DO YOU UNDERSTAND?'"

"Yeah," she grunts. She still hasn't quite caught her breath.

"Good." Paulo seems satisfied. "Now get out of here. I don't want to see your faces for the rest of the day. Send Drew in instead." The two of us turn to leave. "Oh, and tell your people that if anyone talks to the press about what happened here I will personally call Hutch and give him the real version myself. Don't think I'm joking. I do not want my name and studio in *Hollywood Nation* due to child's play." I wince.

I push open the door to the waiting room and the two of us limp out. Drew hurries over to Sky, who sobs on his shoulder. She's always been good at crying on command.

"Are you okay?" Liz whispers. I nod. Rodney shoulders one side of me and ushers us out the gym door onto the sidewalk. I notice Madison hasn't taken her eyes off me. Rodney opens the car door and motions for me to get in. Nadine doesn't say anything till we pull away.

"ARE YOU INSANE?" she shrieks. I burst into tears.

"Lay off, Nadine." Liz hands me a tissue to wipe the blood off my lip.

"Please don't tell Mom," I beg. "I'm so ashamed."

Nadine purses her lips. "I have to. Someone's going to tell the press."

"Someone meaning Madison," I quip. Nadine and Liz look at each other. "Come on, you two, you must suspect her a little bit," I argue. "Remember when I tripped over a wire on set and bruised my knee and it got twisted into that story in *Hollywood Nation* about a fight I had with Sky? And after Hutch yelled at me for flubbing the 'traitor' line on the first take, it was mentioned on *The Insider* yesterday as a sign that Hutch doubts my abilities. Plus, any time something happens, Madison is standing right there. How could you not notice?"

"It is a little odd," Nadine admits. "But forget Madison for the moment. Let's talk about you. No more fighting on set or off! That's not like you to fly off the handle!" I hang my head. "I know I sound like Laney, but you don't need the extra negative attention right now. Let's just finish this crazy movie and get back to *Family Affair*." Nadine shakes her head. "I never thought I'd see the day when I thought that place was normal."

My face feels warm and I stare at the car floor in embarrassment. Nadine is right — I'm not acting like myself at all. I need to get back in control. "What was everyone talking about when you were waiting for Sky and me?" I ask, changing the subject.

"Oh, just Nadine's obvious attraction to Paulo," Liz says.

Nadine glares at her. "Actually, we were talking about our picks for the Hutch Adams title," she says, changing the subject.

"You mean everyone but you did," Liz points out. "You're so secretive."

"I don't want anyone cribbing my idea," Nadine says defensively, turning away to answer her cell phone.

Liz rolls her eyes. "You never want to share anything. I'm glad you didn't play in my sandbox as a kid."

I reach over Liz for my white leather Tod bag and fumble around until I find my Sidekick.

Liz groans. "Don't tell me you're texting Austin again! I thought you said he wasn't mad at you?"

"He's not. I think. I'm just saying hi." I smile sheepishly. I can't get anything past Liz.

"Say hi in person," Nadine offers, shutting her cell. "That was Hank. Hutch canceled production today. Apparently someone leaked the coffeehouse confession scene onto the Internet."

"Oh no!" Liz freaks. "I found the location for that scene last week. I suggested Witch's Brew and Daniella said I was brilliant! Now we're going to have to move it again."

"That scene has the best dialogue in the whole movie," I chime in. It's in the coffee shop that Carly and Donovan learn their parents are in on the nasty superhuman plot and have been preparing us since birth to become the military arm of an evil international empire.

I wonder who leaked the script? It certainly wasn't Hutch. Since gossip about his recent on-set behavior has become public, Hutch has done everything he can to fix his image. He even let an *EW* reporter on set last week to follow him around.

"I could hear Hutch in the background," Nadine says. "He was screaming, 'I'm going to find out who did this and they're going to pay!'"

"Watch someone accuse me of the leak," I say darkly. "That's all I'll need to make my situation on set even worse."

"That's not going to happen," Nadine soothes. "Besides, Hank said Hutch is so upset, he's going to rewrite the dialogue and make it ten times better. Look on the bright side — this means you have the afternoon off."

I have the afternoon off, I realize. I shut my Sidekick. "That means I can make Austin's charity game!"

"Yep. Think you can handle visiting Clark without decking anyone, Rocky?"

"I think so." I laugh. "Rodney, make a U-turn. We're got a game to catch."

FRIDAY 7/6
NOTE TO SELF:

Buy Paulo "sorry" gift
Order Tea & Elixir cart for crew 2 thank them 4 putting up with U
Upcoming Events:
Mexicana premiere with Drew — Sun. @ 6
Dooney & Bourke party at Shelter — Sun. @ 9
Phone Interview with *EW* about *FA* — Mon. @ 2 pm

Matty's first scene — Tuesday!!! GET HIM PRESENT.

TWELVE: *Sweet Charity*

"So when I'm punching the agent in the face do you think my expression should be like this, or this?" Rodney asks as we ascend the packed bleachers at the Clark High School field. I tilt the lid on the red Clark baseball hat Austin gave me and watch Rodney's face change from a terrifying scowl to an ice-cold stare. For a person who trained exclusively for stunts, he's surprisingly expressive.

"The first one," I answer, quickly lowering my head again.

"That's what I thought." Rodney shovels a fistful of the caramel popcorn we bought from the Clark Snack Shack into his mouth. "Paulo thinks I look terrifying in rehearsals," he mumbles. "Do you think I look terrifying?"

"You're definitely good at being intimidating." I grin, taking in Rodney's massive frame, bald head, and dark shades. Maybe that's why, thankfully, nobody has approached us. I do blend in with my outfit: Gap jeans and a black boat-neck sweater with my hair in a ponytail under the cap. Besides, if Tom Cruise, one of the most recognizable stars in the world, can check out a game and not cause a commotion, why can't I?

"KAITLIN BURKE, WHAT ARE YOU DOING HERE?" Principal Pearson screams.

Then again, Tom Cruise didn't trick the entire cheering section into thinking he was someone else for three months.

I nervously bite my lip as a red-faced, heavyset woman wearing a red Clark sweatshirt and khakis barrels through a row of students to get to me. The bleachers are packed. Austin's game must be sold out. OH GOD. Is she going to make me leave because I don't have a ticket? I was planning on making a sizable donation to the cause. A hush grows over our section. "Isn't that Kaitlin Burke?" I hear someone nearby whisper.

"I thought it was you!" Principal P. squeals as she gives me a bear hug. I guess she's not mad. "How have you been?"

I struggle to get some air before answering. "Great," I reply warmly. Principal P. was the only school official in on my charade and she was incredibly nice to me. She's a Family Fanatic (our word for über fans of *FA*).

"I'm sorry you couldn't finish your term," she says apologetically. "The parents association fought me."

I smile. "I understand. It was time for me to leave anyway. I hope its okay I'm here now." I cover my eyes to block the sun. I was in such a hurry, I left my black Gucci sunglasses in the car. "I know students are allowed to donate however much they want to pay for their ticket," I whisper. "I'd like to pay one thousand for mine." I hand over the check I made out in the car.

"A thousand dollars!" Principal P. says in astonishment. She clutches the check tightly. "Wait till I announce this over the loudspeaker on Monday!"

"Oh, if you wouldn't mind, I'd like to keep the donation anonymous," I beg.

Principal P. winks. "Sure thing. It will be our secret." Principal P. chuckles and wipes the sweat from her brow. "So have you gotten any *FA* scripts yet for the new season? The chat room I was in last night said that Paige is going to be in a coma after the car crash!"

Before I can answer, someone plops down in front of me.

"I can't believe you made it!" squeals Austin's sister, Hayley. "Hi, Principal Pearson!" she adds.

Principal P. looks disappointed. "Oh, hi, Hayley." She stands up. "I should go, Kaitlin. I need to make the rounds, you know. Thank you again for your, uh, ticket donation." I nod, looking around Principal P. to see what everyone is screaming about.

Rodney clears his throat. "Clark scored a goal against the faculty. Frankly, I think it's unfair for the team to play the teachers. They have an advantage, you know." I look down at the field and see Austin give his muddy teammates a high five. Pay attention, Kaitlin!

"I told Riley and Prue you would totally come if you could get off work, but it's not like you can take a sick day," I hear Hayley say. She motions to two shy girls sitting next to her. I shake Riley's sweaty hand and autograph Prue's shaking wrist, then ask Hayley what I really need to know.

"Do you know if your brother is mad at me?"

Hayley's blue eyes grow wide. "He's acting so weird. He wouldn't tell us how his set visit with you went. All he can talk about is this stupid charity match."

Gulp. "Where are your mom and dad?" I search the stands and see them a few rows back. Mrs. Meyers waves, but Mr. Meyers is so wrapped up in the game, he doesn't see me. It's just as well. He probably hates me after last Friday night.

I look at the field in time to see Austin run off it. He looks sweaty and dirty and tired and, well, completely adorable. As Austin approaches the bench I see his ex, Lori, standing on the sidelines with a towel and a bottle of Gatorade. Austin takes them from her and smiles. Hey!

"Ever since Austin started dating the real you, Lori's been all over him again," Hayley confides over another round of cheers.

"So I noticed," I reply stiffly, trying not to overact as I watch Lori giggle wildly at something Austin said. Concentrate on the game, Kaitlin. Austin jogs back to the middle of the field.

Austin has explained lacrosse to me before, but it's all a bit hazy now. I know he's an attackman, which means he's the guy who gets the goals, but beyond that, I'm lost. Rodney somehow knows a little about the sport, which he's happy to share after I've sent Hayley down to the Snack Shack to buy out the brownies the Key Club is selling.

"Austin's got great stick skills!" he marvels. "You see how he made that save? He's a natural."

"He is?" I feel proud watching him run down the torn-up field cradling the stick, dodging his opponents. I pay strict attention to the rest of the game, even turning off my cell phone and Sidekick (Nadine and Laney are going to kill me) so that I can watch Austin's every move. Well, when I'm not greeting students, that is. I have such guilt over my disguise at Clark that I don't let Rodney turn away anyone who wants my autograph or a picture. By the fourth quarter, I've seen almost everyone I knew, including my old history teacher, Mr. Klein, who still looks peeved that I didn't hand in my extra-credit paper.

With the score twelve to six, and two minutes left in the game, I'm standing on my feet screaming along with the rest of the school and Rodney, who is jumping so hard the stands seem to be swaying. When the final buzzer sounds and the students have officially beat Coach Connor and the rest of the faculty, I hug everyone around me. One guy holds on so tight that Rodney has to pry him off. According to Hayley's bookkeeping, Austin scored one goal, two saves, and one assist.

People pour out of the bleachers and descend upon the field to join in the celebration. I see Lori push her way towards Austin, but thankfully the crowd is too large for her to get to him. I watch Austin and the other lacrosse players hoist a large jug full of Gatorade over Coach Connor's head. Ice rains down on Austin's dictatorial coach, and he actually laughs.

"Aren't you going down there?" Rodney asks. The two of us seem to be the last ones in the bleachers. I shake my head.

"I think I'll let Austin enjoy the moment." I watch Austin take the mic and hush the large crowd.

"Thanks to everyone for coming out today to help us raise money for our trip," Austin's voice echoes across the field. "Man, you guys are generous. The total isn't official yet, but it looks like we've raised over three thousand dollars. Thank you!" A loud roar erupts from the crowd.

A camera flashes in our direction and I look down to see a few people taking pictures of me instead of the jubilation on the field.

"Your being here is definitely going to make the papers," Rodney growls, staring at one of the amateur photographers.

I shrug. "It was worth it," I add as the team finally leaves the revelers behind and heads up the path to the gym to get to the locker rooms. As they pass by the bleachers, one of Austin's teammates points to me. My heart seems to stop altogether as he turns and bounds up the steps towards me. Rodney slips away and parks himself at the bottom of the section to keep the spies at bay.

"Hey," I squeak as Austin stops short at the bench below mine. I stand perfectly still with my hands clenched in my jean pockets, trying to think of the perfect supportive girlfriend thing to say. "Great game," I blurt. UGH. Lame.

Austin takes a swig from his water bottle. "I didn't expect to see you here." He's out of breath.

"At the last minute, I got the afternoon off," I explain. "I'm glad I got to see you play. You — you've got great stick skills," I stammer, trying to repeat what Rodney told me. "And that assist you made in the fourth quarter was amazing."

Austin smirks. "Since when do you know lacrosse-speak?"

"I've been studying," I lie. "Today I know you scored a goals, two saves, and one assist."

Austin laughs. "Keep going. It's going to take more than knowing today's score to get you out of the hot water you're in, Burke."

"I knew you were mad about that scene I did with Drew!" I say accusingly. "Why didn't you say anything?"

"Thinking about Drew kissing you was driving me crazy," Austin admits. "But I hate fighting over the phone. Lori and I did that all the time and it drove me nuts. I think it's better to talk about things face-to-face, like we tried doing last week." Austin wipes the sweat from his drenched hair. "With your hectic schedule, I wasn't sure when that would be so I kept talking about the charity game to keep us from talking about the real problem here."

"Oh." I pull my hands inside the sleeves of my sweater. "Can I talk first? I want to apologize for jumping down your throat the other day. When you started talking Hollywood with me, I got bent out of shape."

"I was trying to help you." Austin takes a seat on his bench and I sit alone on mine. The sun has slipped behind the gathering clouds, and I shiver. "Has anyone ever told you you're not very good at taking advice?" he asks.

"Occasionally." I think of Nadine and Laney. "I wanted to finish our discussion after I shot the scene. But you bailed out of there without even saying goodbye."

"Can you blame me?" Austin asks indignantly. "I wasn't going to sit there and applaud. Who wants to watch his girl-friend suck face with another guy?"

I think of how I felt to watch Lori near Austin again. Truthfully, I wanted to rip her to pieces. "Nobody," I agree. "But I had no idea Drew was going to pull a stunt like that. We didn't have a kiss scheduled. Do you really think I would have invited you to watch me shoot a love scene?"

HOLLYWOOD SECRET NUMBER TWELVE: You've probably heard actors claim this and I can attest that it's really true: filming love scenes is not a romantic experience at all. On-screen, a make-out session looks like three minutes of pure heaven. But it's not. Those three minutes took HOURS to film. HOURS. Imagine lying there, in some cases, half-naked (though I'm not talking about myself, since I have a "no nudity" clause in my contracts), with a camera inches from your face, a crew of twenty standing around you, and a director yelling things like, "Use more lip, Kaitlin! Turn your head slightly to the left. Now hold it! Drew, put your hand on Kaitlin's hip, stay there, and action!" Then you have to do the shot again, from several more angles. It's too technical and awkward to be romantic, even if the guy you're kissing is cute. And don't get me started about the guys I've locked lips with who've skipped the Listerine. Ewww . . .

Austin grabs his head with his hands and groans like I'm killing him. "I'm sick of fighting. We've been fighting on and off for over a week."

I slide down next to him. "I know. I don't want to fight anymore either. I'm going to make things up to you," I promise. "I'm taking you on the best date EVER."

He looks at me skeptically. "When?"

"August twelfth."

He laughs loudly. "That's a month away! Is that your next day off?"

"No, it's the date of the Teen Titan Awards. I'm hosting with Drew." Austin raises an eyebrow. "But you're going to be my date," I add.

"Seriously?" He's intrigued, I can tell. "Do I have to, like, escort you down the red carpet or something?"

I think for a minute. "Yeah, and you get to be my date at all the parties that night and at the cool gift suite they usually have backstage. There's a lot of perks to sticking with me through this lousy movie shoot," I point out. "I'm also booking you for the Hollywood Girl Awards, which are coming up. They're honoring me and I want you to be there."

He touches my cheek. I close my eyes and enjoy the warmth of his hand. Who cares if my cheek is probably black and blue from Sky's jab?

"Is that a reason to date you, Burke?" Austin asks. "To go

to awards shows and swanky parties? You should know me better than that."

"You're not like that, I know," I say softly. "I just want you to realize how much I want you in my life. This is the first time I've hosted anything before, and I want you there."

He leans forward and grabs my hands in his own, which are rough and dirty. "Then it's a date," he says.

I lean into his chest and he wraps his arms around me tightly. The warmth from his body seeps through my sweater, and I don't feel cold anymore.

"I heard from Principal P. that someone made an anonymous thousand-dollar donation to our lacrosse camp fund," Austin says. "You wouldn't happen to know anyone who would have that kind of money to donate, would you?"

"Not a clue," I mumble into Austin's chest.

"Well, if you find out who did it, tell them I said thanks," Austin whispers. "Now about that kiss with Drew," Austin continues. "Let me show you how it should have been done." I look up and Austin kisses me softly on my bruised lips. My whole body melts like marshmallows in hot cocoa. I guess Austin was just the medicine I needed.

FRIDAY 7/6
NOTE TO SELF:

Hook A up w/Nadine to get duds for Hollywood Girl party and TT Awards. :)

SCRIPT CONTINUED

115 INT. ROB'S BEDROOM

We PAN ACROSS Rob's ultra-neat bedroom from the closet to the bed, where Rob is sleeping. Carly peeks out of the closet and hurries across the room to the edge of Rob's bed.

CARLY
Rob. Wake up. It's me.

ROB
Carly! Are you okay? We've been looking everywhere for you!

CARLY
Rob, you've got to listen closely. Get dressed. You've got to leave with me before they come after you too.

ROB
Carly, you need help. Let us help you.

CARLY
Us? Rob, don't tell me they've gotten to you.
(She begins looking for an escape as Rob talks.)

ROB

You don't have to be afraid anymore, Carly. Just come downstairs and talk to Mom and Dad. Tell them you were wrong. Everything will go back to normal.

CARLY

Listen to yourself. They're brainwashing you! They're making you think the changes that are happening to our bodies and minds are a good thing. Do you think normal people can leap across buildings, Rob?

ROB

They're doing this for the greater good. You're missing what's at stake here.

CARLY

(backs up to the window and tries to pry it open behind her without Rob seeing)
There's still time, Rob. Leave with me.

ROB

I'm sorry, Carly. You obviously don't get it and you've left me no choice.
(yelling)
MOM! DAD! MRS. MURPHY! SHE'S HERE!

THIRTEEN: *Matty's Debut*

"There's still time, Rob," I whisper breathlessly as I try to pry the window open behind me. "Leave with me."

Matty stands across from me wearing a long-sleeved blue flannel and gray sweatpants. His blond hair has the perfect bed-head look. His expression is steely. "I'm sorry, Carly," he says coldly. "You obviously don't get it and you've left me no choice."

Wow, Matty sounds so convincing! My eyes widen and I express a range of emotions quickly — shock that my brother is betraying me, hurt that he doesn't believe me, fear that I'm about to be captured. I know what I have to do. I pull the fake window up and place one leg over the frame, pretending to look down at the ground, which is supposed to be three stories away. It's actually only six feet down. I can see the air mattress and two spotters waiting for my fall. I look back at Matty with a look of horror. He points at me.

"MOM! DAD!" he yells at the top of his lungs. "MRS. MURPHY! SHE'S HERE!"

Footsteps approach rapidly and seconds later the door to Rob's room is being rammed open by two large men who look like they were borrowed from World Wrestling. One of them is Rodney.

"STOP HER!" he bellows menacingly as he charges towards me.

With one last fleeting look at Matty, or should I say Rob, I throw my other leg over the frame, duck my head, and jump. I hit the soft pillow and bounce up and down for a moment, enjoying the adrenaline rush.

"EXCELLENT work, you two!" Hutch says through his megaphone. The dark-haired spotter offers me his hand and I grab it and jump off the mattress. I walk around the fake exterior wall behind Rob's bedroom to the front, where the three-walled two-story set is constructed down to the tiniest detail (there's a half-eaten veggie burger sitting on Rob's nightstand). Hutch and the crew are in one corner and my parents are congratulating Matty in another. While the crew sets up the next angle to be shot for the scene, I run over and give Matty a fierce bear hug.

"I'm so proud of you," I gush. "You were unbelievable in that scene. I seriously feared for my safety."

Matty blushes. "Did you really think I was good?" he asks anxiously.

"You were great," I reply truthfully. "After that scene, I'd act alongside you any day." Matty smiles shyly.

"Matty, you had such inner strength," my mom marvels.

"It was definitely a leading-man moment," my dad seconds.

Matt takes a swig of water from the bottle he's holding. "It was nothing really," he says, sounding more confident. "I knew if my sister was going to betray the organization I loved, I had to take her down." He stands perfectly still as the makeup artist applies powder to his shiny nose. She turns to me and adds more powder and another swab of pale pink lip gloss.

"What about me?" Rodney says as he joins us. "Was I intimidating?" He seems very excited. This was Rodney's first scene too.

"Definitely," I agree. "I jumped, didn't I?" He punches me softly in the arm. "How are you doing, Mr. B., Mrs. B.?" Rodney asks my parents. "Have you been to Matty's trailer yet?" While my folks have been to the set numerous times already, even if it's just to drop off some new tabloid story, this is the first time they're seeing Matt's home away from home.

Hutch interrupts us, putting an arm each around Matt and me and I feel myself tense. "We're not going to do another take, guys," he says, tugging on his goatee. "I think we have all the setups we need for this shot. You can take a well-deserved forty-minute break while we set up the library set. I want to look over the script one more time and see if anything needs tweaking." What? Hutch sounds bizarrely cheerful. "Enjoy it and keep that motivation pumping, Kaitlin and Matt," he adds. "We'll see you over there." Hutch winks at my mother, shakes my dad's hand, lowers his trademark shades, and is gone.

"He doesn't act like he hates you, Katie-Kins," my dad whispers encouragingly. "*Hollywood Nation* must have it wrong."

My face darkens. Mom gave me the article Dad is referring to when I arrived home from Austin's charity game. When I read it, I actually cried. I know better than anyone that a lot of these stories are made up, but this one was so on the mark with what I've been feeling lately that I couldn't stop myself. The "source" in the story said that the reason Hutch has been so difficult on set is that he feels he made a huge mistake in casting me over Sky to play Carly. The story went on to explain that Hutch thought I was a bad actor and difficult to work with. Laney was furious. "These types of articles could ruin your renewed likeability factor!" she yelled. I wonder if Hutch has seen the article. Usually when an article about him appears in the press, his mood turns from icy to downright blizzard conditions.

"You really don't know why Hutch is being so complimentary?" Matt asks. I shake my head. "Haven't you noticed the *Premiere* reporter sitting next to him all morning?"

I look over at Hutch, who is deep in conversation with Daniella and Liz and a redhead I don't recognize. She steps back and begins writing furiously in her notebook. Oh.

"Let's see your trailer, Matty," Mom suggests. She gathers up her new dark brown leather Miu Miu purse, her magazines (she hasn't mentioned any new stories — yet), and her large bottle of Fiji water, and heads to the waiting golf cart that will bring us back to the trailers.

"We don't have to go there, Mom." Matt looks alarmed. "Let's just go back to Kaitlin's trailer instead. It's closer."

"Nonsense." Dad pats Matt on the back. "I want to see the piece of machinery you're calling home these days. Do you happen to know what cylinder the engine is?"

I try to get Matt's attention as we drive across the lot to the parked trailers to reassure him that his trailer is fine, but he won't look at me. When we pull up outside the sixty-five-foot Honeywagon, Mom actually whistles.

"This is bigger than Kaitlin's!" She steps nimbly out of the cart in her three-inch spiky black sandals. Dad steadies her with his available arm and the two walk directly towards the first door they see.

"Uh, no, guys, you don't understand," Matt blurts out, racing to stop them before they open the door. "That one isn't mine. I'm the seventh door down."

"Seventh?" Mom is confused.

"He shares the trailer, Mom," I explain. "There's ten actors in this one and each has their own dressing room."

"Oh," Mom says quietly.

Matt takes her by the arm and leads her to his room. He opens the metal door and we peer inside the tiny space. There's just enough room for a desk, mirror, and chair. The four of us, not counting Rodney, can barely squeeze inside.

"It's very nice for your first trailer, dear," Mom says lightly. She holds her head stiffly as if to avoid looking around.

"Thanks." Matt looks miserable. I put my arm on his shoulder, but he pushes it off.

"Where's the bathroom?" Dad asks, feeling the wall for a hidden door. "I should go before the next scene."

"Can we go to Kaitlin's trailer," Matt begs. "Please? That's really my trailer too. I can't fit all of my stuff in here."

Everyone is quiet on the ride over, but the silence is broken when we pull up to my trailer and hear Nadine and Liz yelling. Matt perks up immediately and bolts for the door.

"Were you two fighting?" he demands excitedly as the rest of us quickly follow him inside.

Nadine and Liz's sour expressions give it away. "What happened?" I ask nervously. Liz's eyes narrow as she looks from me to my parents.

"Could the three of us have a moment in private please?" she answers frostily, leading the way from our crowded kitchen and living area to the bedroom. Nadine crosses her arms and marches ahead of me. I shut the door and turn on my CD player to keep the others from listening in.

"What's wrong?" I thought now that Austin and I made up, my personal life would be drama-free for a while.

Nadine glares at Liz. "I am sick and tired of Liz thinking she's above doing assistant work," she spits out angrily. "Wardrobe just yelled at me for not bringing back your outfit yesterday. That was something I asked Liz to do!"

"I was helping Daniella scout a new location for the coffee shop scene," Liz yells. "I thought that was more important than returning a pair of ripped jeans."

"You show up late for work, go for a long coffee break with Madison, and spend the afternoon with Daniella," Nadine charges. "When exactly do you think you're doing assistant work, Liz?"

Liz shakes her head and looks at her pink Converse sneakers. "I'm not Kaitlin's real assistant," Liz seethes. "Kaitlin knows I'm here to work with Daniella."

"But Kaitlin's paying you, which means you're supposed to actually help out," Nadine retorts. "Or are you so rich you forgot about your paycheck?"

"I'm sick of you treating me like your intern," Liz complains. "Why am I the one who has to arrange Kaitlin's weekly birds-of-paradise flower arrangement and get her Coffee Bean & Tea Leaf fix and pick up her dry-cleaning?"

"I can't trust you enough to do anything else, that's why," Nadine replies bitterly. "I worked my way through college and I've been assisting Kaitlin for a few years so that I can pay for business school." She glances at me. "And I care about this job and work hard to do it well. Why are you here? So you can tell Daddy you have a real job? You're just a spoiled rich kid who thinks the world owes her something. Well, you know what? It doesn't." Nadine's face is almost the same color as her hair.

Liz lunges forward, but I hold on to her Pucci t-shirt with my right arm. WHOA. I've never heard either of them so angry. Before they started working together, they always got along.

"How dare you talk to me like that?" Liz counters. "It's not my fault you're stuck working as Kaitlin's slave."

"Slave?" I jump in, getting upset. "I guess that spa weekend I gave Nadine in Palm Springs last month was torture."

HOLLYWOOD SECRET NUMBER THIRTEEN: Nadine and Liz's job isn't a picnic, but it isn't all chores either. Nadine has some pretty great perks as a celebrity personal assistant — a nice paycheck, first-class flights anywhere she goes with me, her own hotel room, killer freebies (Jacob & Co. recently gave her some pretty nice bling that's usually reserved for celebrities), and a sideline view to all of the Hollywood action. I should remind them that not all personal assistants have it this easy. Sky makes her ever-changing assistant do heinous things like pop her zits (EWW!). A teen country music star I know makes his assistant run all over town to find Air Force One sneakers (he never wears the same pair more than twice). Another acquaintance makes his assistant have his Evian purified by a shaman before he'll drink it. And one of my married costars on *FA* makes his assistant, um, pay his girlfriend's bills on the sly.

Liz sighs. "I'm sorry, Kates. I didn't mean that. I got carried away."

"Me too," Nadine grumbles.

"I don't want to lose either of you," I plead. "Now that you've both said everything you've been holding in, maybe you can just make up?" I suggest hopefully.

Nadine and Liz continue to glare at each other. "I'm a professional," Nadine says stiffly. "Working together won't be a problem."

"Whatever she said," Liz mutters.

Well, neither actually apologized, but I guess this is a start.

Liz opens the door to the living room and walks out without looking back. She picks up her Sidekick. "According to Nadine's tight schedule, I'm supposed to get you coffee right now," Liz says to me. "What do you want?"

"I'll take a Mocha Frappuccino," Matty calls out from the couch where he's watching *Dr. Phil*. Mom sits next to him reading the latest issue of *Hollywood Nation*. "With extra whipped cream."

Liz and I look at each other.

"This came for you, Katie-Kins, while you were inside." Dad holds out two sheets of white paper. "It's tomorrow's schedule."

"I'll bet it is," I grumble. "Can one of you double-check this?" I ask Nadine and Liz.

Liz sighs loudly. "I can't believe you still think Maddy is trying to sabotage you —"

Nadine snatches the paper. "I'll double-check it," she interrupts. "I'm starting to think there have been one too many mistakes involving Madison for them all to be accidents." I smile gratefully.

"Why would someone give you a fake call sheet?" Dad asks.

"Madison hates Kaitlin." Matt yawns. "So do Sky and Drew. And Hutch half the time." I glare at Matt.

"You mean the *Nation* article is true?" Dad looks confused. "I heard Hutch was a screamer and bad with staying on schedule, but I can't believe anyone would hate our Katie-Kat."

"You knew all that and didn't tell me?" I'm incredulous. "Why would you let me work with someone like that?"

"You've always admired him, sweetie, and Mom thought the role was good for your career," Dad says gently. "You're a fighter! We knew you could handle him. Besides, this is your first two-million-dollar paycheck. Isn't the headache worth it?"

I don't know if I should laugh or cry. Before I can do either, Mom lets out a small sob.

"Who the hell is Hayley Meyers?" she asks, holding up an article with a picture of Austin and me. "And why is she talking to *Hollywood Nation* about your relationship? Or about *that boy's* ex-girlfriend?"

I look from Liz to Nadine, since they still won't glance at each other, and try not to laugh. Hayley. The poor kid probably got cold-called and didn't know what hit her.

"Seriously, Katie-Kat, do you think this relationship is worth it?" Mom starts, but she's interrupted by Nadine's walkie-talkie.

"Kaitlin Burke. Matt Burke. You're needed on the library set in ten," Hank shouts cheerfully.

I've never been so happy to get back to set. "I've got to go," I say quickly, snatching the magazine from her hands to read the article on the golf cart ride over. I gather my cue cards and motion to Rodney to get the door.

"Kaitlin, I'm talking to you," Mom persists. "We need to discuss getting the confidentiality agreements signed by the Meyers. What if the whole family is trying to make money off you?"

I grab Matty's arm and race out the door. I've had enough drama for one day.

WEDNESDAY 7/11
NOTE TO SELF:

Thurs. Calltime 8 PM — Canyon Creek Park
Fri.-Sun. On location in San Diego, calltime 6 AM — (PACK SUITCASE! Have Nadine check hotel res. Does hotel have masseuse???)
7/21 Hollywood Girl bash

fourteen: *Your Typical* Hollywood Girl

"Kaitlin, where are the three-carat diamond earrings we borrowed for you to wear?" Mom demands.

I'm so happy to be cuddled next to Austin in the black stretch limo that I completely forgot anyone else was here. I look across the aisle at Mom, who has her right eyebrow raised menacingly. I slowly reach up and touch my unaccessorized earlobe. Uh-oh.

"Rodney, turn the car around," Mom commands. "I can't believe you forgot your earrings!" she scolds. Her own diamonds chandelier earrings sway as she shakes her head.

I smile sheepishly, but I'm at a loss for words. Liz and Nadine are in the dog house so I didn't expect them to pipe up, but my other limo mates — Dad, Matt, Austin, and Rodney — don't jump to my defense either. I guess Mom can be pretty scary.

I've been so looking forward to tonight. Not only because I'm being honored by *Hollywood Girl* magazine as one of their five women of the year, but also, and most important, because I get to spend the whole evening with Austin. Even though we've been speaking and e-mailing every day, I've been counting down the hours till I could see Austin (and drool over him in a suit). He's been on a family vacation in San Francisco. He brought me back a cool t-shirt and Hayley got me a box of saltwater taffy. Austin said his mom grounded her post-vacay for three weeks for talking to the press. Poor girl.

But all thoughts of Austin flew out the window when Rodney and I got home and found Mom, hair half-done, still in her True Religion capri-length jeans, yelling at Nadine and Liz, who had left the set early to pick up my gorgeous, one-of-a-kind white chiffon and silver sequined dress. Laney was fighting with them too — she was screaming obscenities over the speaker phone.

"You two are supposed to have Kaitlin's back!" Mom said frostily as she paced back and forth while Nadine and Liz looked on, white-faced. "Instead, you're adding to her problems!"

"WHAT WERE YOU TWO THINKING?" Laney yelled over the roar of the highway she was probably speeding down. "YOU *NEVER* DISCUSS YOUR BOSS IN FRONT OF OTHER PEOPLE ... WHAT? ARE YOU TALKING TO ME? WHAT DO YOU MEAN I CAN'T MAKE A U-TURN HERE?"

"Laney, we didn't discuss work in front of anyone but Kaitlin," Liz squeaked as Mom glared at her. "Someone must have overheard us fighting that day in her trailer."

"Please! It's obvious you two haven't been getting along," Mom snapped hoarsely. "No one had to overhear your conversation to know that."

"What's going on?" I demanded wearily. The three of them jumped. I don't think any of them realized I was home yet.

"Well, tell her." Mom folded her arms across her chest and motioned to Nadine and Liz.

"There's an article about all of us in this week's *Hollywood Nation*," Nadine said quietly, her eyes on our Italian marble–tiled floor instead of my face.

"We're so sorry, Kates." Liz stepped towards me as Mom smacked the magazine down on the black granite-topped kitchen island. Rodney and I looked at each other and rushed over to read it.

KAITLIN BURKE'S ASSISTANT BLUES

Family Affair star Kaitlin Burke is making enemies even inside her own camp. Sources close to the star, who is currently shooting Hutch Adams's as yet untitled actioner, say her assistants are ready to walk off the job. Just last week, executive assistant Nadine Cobb and recently hired best pal turned gofer, Liz Mendes, were caught bickering on set over their boss's increasingly outrageous demands. "Liz was saying how over she was of picking up after Kaitlin's wannabe actor/brother Matthew and Nadine was saying how tired she was of making Starbucks coffee runs three times a day," says the source. The pair reportedly fought over who would have to get Kaitlin's green tea and who would stick around set to have lunch with the star. "By the end of the heated argument, both were saying how much they hate their gigs." Looks like Kaitlin Burke has another war raging — in her own backyard!

When I finished reading, I was too shocked to say anything. They would never talk about me to the press. Would they? "I thought we settled this," I said quietly, too hurt to be angry.

"W-we did," Liz stuttered. "Kates, you have to believe me, I mean us." Liz grabbed Nadine's arm in sudden solidarity and the two clung to each other. "We would never say those things. You know why we're fighting."

"Madison is behind this," Nadine said firmly. "I saw her hanging outside Kaitlin's trailer that afternoon but didn't think anything of it. She must have leaked our fight to the magazine."

"That's why she asked me if I was getting along with you!" Liz hit her hand against her forehead. "I thought it was weird when she asked me if I ever felt like your intern. I can't believe I trusted her! I feel so stupid. I'm sorry I didn't believe you, Kates," Liz added. I just nodded.

"Laney, we have to go after this girl," Nadine pleaded to the phone. "I've been doing some digging the past few days and I'm convinced that Madison is behind all these bad tabloid stories."

"NADINE, WE CAN DISCUSS THIS LATER," Laney yelled. "A COP IS PULLING *ME* OVER. THE NERVE! I'LL SEE YOU THERE, KAIT —" The line went dead.

Mom snatched the magazine from my hands. "I'm not wasting any more time talking about this. Kaitlin and I have to get ready. The limo will be here in two hours, right, Nadine?"

"Yes," Nadine whispered. Mom stomped up the stairs to slip into her pale pink empire gown.

"I'm sorry we didn't listen to you about Madison. Especially me. I can't believe I sided with her over my best friend." Liz looked practically in tears.

"We're going to prove we didn't do this," Nadine added. "You'll see."

I wanted to believe they weren't bashing me to the press. But the three of us were the only ones in the room when they had their fight. Mom wasn't forgiving anyone. She didn't talk at all while she got ready. Neither did Matty, who wasn't thrilled about being referred to as a "wannabe actor."

With everything going on, is it any surprise I forgot the jewels? Thankfully, after the quick detour home, we arrive at the Hollywood Roosevelt Hotel in less than a half hour, including traffic. I powder my nose to control shine and slip the compact back into my Tod's Girelli pochette. Then I'm ready to hit the red carpet with fellow winner Mina Burrows, escorted by her P.A. boyfriend.

As Austin and I walk the line together, I can't stop smiling. Austin may be nervous, but he's acting like a complete pro, steering me through the cameramen and answering questions from the interviewers (I almost fainted when

Austin replied that his favorite things about me are my "inner strength — and killer eyes"). I'm the one having trouble talking to the press! I can't concentrate. All I can think about is the gentle pressure of Austin's hand on the small of my back and the secret wink he gave me when freakishly tall and skinny Larry the Liar asked to take a picture of me solo.

Before I know it, we're being ushered through the restored lobby of the 1920s hotel and outside past the palm trees to the Tropicana Bar where everyone else, including Laney, is waiting. A dozen round tables surround the pool and the low-lit bar area. Each "reserved" table is covered with a taffeta tablecloth in *Hollywood Girl*'s signature color, crimson red. Small votive candles, surrounded by rose petals, light up the appetizer (a walnut and pear salad). Each place setting has a red brochure, which, as I know from past years as a guest, contains the five winners' pictures along with copies of our profiles from the current issue. At each winner's tables, there are poster-size pictures from our articles. In my shot, I'm laughing at the Celebrity Cares Circus, handing out cotton candy to needy kids from the Watts section of L.A. I can tell Austin is still nervous hanging with the likes of Scarlett Johansson, so I try to distract him by pointing out hotel landmarks, like the David Hockney mural on the bottom of the still pool.

"That's nice, but more importantly, what is this award for?" Austin's eyes twinkle mischievously. He knows as well as I do this is no Oscar.

"Well, according to Laney, *Hollywood Girl* looks for stars who are likable, have great projects, and have overcome some sort of obstacle," I explain.

"You mean like enrolling at a public high school as someone else?" he teases.

"Yeah, like that." I lightly punch him in the arm and cringe as a flashbulb goes off to capture the moment. We're almost at our table. "It's going to be a long night if they're still fighting," I whisper, referring to the tag team of Mom and Laney versus Nadine and Liz. After the storm I walked into at my house, I quickly called Austin to warn him about the possibly tense evening.

"They'll be fine." Austin hits the table first and pulls out my chair. "Burke, you're forgetting your own celebrity rules," he whispers in my ear. "Rule number one: When in public, never air your dirty laundry."

I laugh. "How could I forget?" I say softly as I sink into my cushioned seat at our VIP table.

"Katie-Kat, finally!" Mom squeals as I place a red silk napkin in my lap. She looks much happier than she was an hour ago. I'm not sure if that's due to the Chocolate Martini she's sipping or the fact that Liz and Nadine are seated as far away from Mom as possible. "Wait till you hear the amazing news Laney has!"

"I just got off the phone with Seth," Laney says breathlessly, talking about my agent, Seth. "You've been asked to be the new face of Fever cosmetics!"

"W-wow," I stammer and grin at Austin. He looks confused. Why am I surprised that he doesn't know his elite and oh-so-expensive ($350 for night cream) cosmetic lines? "Fever is a huge makeup company," I explain. "Hallie Diament did their campaign last year and she had ads in every fashion book, a billboard in Times Square, and a commercial shot by Baz Luhrmann."

HOLLYWOOD SECRET NUMBER FOURTEEN: Real celebrity endorsement deals — and I don't mean stars talking about their favorite watch on *Ellen* in the hopes they'll get a free one delivered to their house the next day — are quite lucrative. (We're talking seven figures! But you didn't hear that from me. Celebrities never reveal how much a company paid them for advertising gigs.) My mom and Seth have always been picky about who they thought was worthy of the "Kaitlin Burke brand," which is why you won't see me hawking zit medication anytime soon. But Fever is a no-brainer: classy, high-end, and popular. Still, if I sign on, I've got to watch my step. If you're caught using a rival brand's product, or you talk about another brand in a magazine, you can get fired. A supermodel I know got canned from her diet soda contract after she was caught on film sipping the enemy's beverage on three separate occasions. And my friend Gina, who was hired by a brand that's known for their all-natural soaps, begged a magazine not to reveal that she used a rival body wash on the set of her new movie.

"So this Fever offer is a good thing, right?" Austin asks.

"Good?" Laney's smile reveals her recently laser-whitened teeth. "Are you kidding? This is huge!" She clinks martini glasses with my mom. "It certainly will help me spin some positive press for you. The only downside, Kaitlin, is that you have to use your next two days off to shoot their fall ads. And then when the Hutch movie wraps in three weeks, they'll want to shoot a commercial before you start production on *FA*, which starts up on August twenty-first," Laney adds.

"That's not a problem," Mom answers for me as a *Hollywood Girl* editor stops by to steal me away for some pictures.

Before the main course of roasted chicken with cranberry chutney is served, I pose with *Hollywood Girl*'s editor-in-chief and the publisher, then take a few more shots with the other recipients before my official duties are done. *Hollywood Girl* doesn't have a formal awards ceremony, but they do hand out little gold statues that look like the Hollywood sign to each of the winners. When I'm finished, I find Liz and Nadine whispering heatedly near the corner of the sleek bar. I stop short and eye them both suspiciously.

"Are you two fighting again?"

"We're not fighting," Nadine promises.

"Good. Where's Austin and Matty?" I look across the pool at our semi-empty table where Mom, Dad, and Laney are deep in conversation

"The bathroom." Liz looks glum. "We want to apologize again for bringing you into the middle of our argument. We should have handled our differences ourselves, which is what we're going to do from now on."

"Just don't ask us what we're up to, okay?" Nadine adds. "We'd rather you not be implicated if anything were to, say, blow up in our faces."

"Um, okay," I laugh. Frankly, I'm just relieved they're speaking again.

"Mina Burrows and her boyfriend have to be the cutest couple ever," Liz gushes, changing the subject. The three of us turn to look at Mina and the tall, dark-haired P.A. slow dancing. Mina is caressing his hair while he's kissing her neck.

Nadine rubs her left eyebrow. "In another minute I'm going to walk over there and tell them to get a room!"

"Leave them alone. They're in love," I say dreamily. Nadine purses her lips.

"I know you, Kaitlin," Nadine chides. "You just like them because Mina is dating a real guy." Liz chuckles. "You never read the tabloids unless your mom makes you and then suddenly you're asking me to pick up Celebrity Insider and asking if there's anything about Mina inside!"

I blush. Okay, maybe I am a little into seeing what happens to another couple in the same situation as my own, but I'm too embarrassed to admit it. "I don't know what you're talking about." I take a sip of my virgin raspberry margarita. Liz and Nadine are so busy laughing that we don't notice Carol Ingram walk over.

"Hello, Kaitlin," Carol says warmly. I don't know how I didn't notice Carol was here. Carol sticks out among the sea of partygoers in their Marc Jacobs and Stella McCartney in her stuffy business attire: gray slacks and a fitted short-sleeved black cashmere sweater. In high heels, she's taller than most of the men here too. "I wanted to come by and congratulate you," she says.

"Thank you," I reply cautiously.

"Girls, would you mind if Kaitlin and I chatted alone for a minute?" she says to Nadine and Liz. They both excuse themselves, but Liz looks back at me worriedly.

"I didn't find out till the last minute that you were being honored." Carol taps her gin and tonic lightly with her short, clear-glossed nails. "I thought Laney was going to keep me in the loop about your publicity." She smiles.

"I'm sorry," I apologize. "The award had nothing to do with the movie so Laney probably forgot to mention it."

Carol stares down at me. "Kaitlin, everything you do during filming has to do with the Hutch movie." Her voice is light, but definitely firm. "I wanted to remind you about that." Oh no.

"Your fight with Sky at the premiere of *Antarctica*, shunning Sky and Drew on set in front of reporters, these are all things that reflect poorly not only on your reputation, but the film's as well."

I'm not sure how to reply. I can't exactly argue with one of the most powerful women in Hollywood, but Carol should know what's really going on. "I hope you don't believe all those things, Carol," I begin gingerly. "I would never do anything to hurt the film. You know how it is with the tabloids. They're so eager to break a story that they'll run with any tip they get, even if it's from a completely unreliable source." I laugh, hoping she'll join in. She doesn't.

"I know I work differently than a lot of people around here, but I believe it's my innovativeness that produces the positive results." I nod nervously. "From what I can tell, everyone else is getting along fine," Carol continues. "Drew is more than willing to be part of the aggressive publicity plan I've outlined. I fear you are the problem."

I look around for Laney to rescue me, but she's nowhere in sight.

"You're a bankable star, Kaitlin. I'd like to see you do more films with Wagman." Carol smiles at Scarlett Johansson as she walks by. "But the way things are going, I think you may run into problems with us. People talk, you know."

Is she threatening me? "Carol, I assure you," I reply firmly as I wave at Scarlett, "the last thing I want is to blow my movie career when it's just getting off the ground."

"Help me make my first publicity project go well here and all will be forgotten."

"I'll do anything," I reply, regretting the words as soon as they escape from my lips. I feel like I've been tricked.

"Good." Carol takes a small sip of her gin and tonic and grins. "Then I won't hear of any problems with you hosting the Teen Titan Awards?"

"Definitely not," I assure her.

"Great, I'll let Drew's people know we're on." Carol pulls her BlackBerry out of her Louis Vuitton bag to e-mail them immediately. "I think the two of you appearing together will give us great press."

"I'm sorry. You mean host together, right?" I can feel a pulse in my forehead as I wait for her answer.

"No, I mean *go* together," she says, emphasizing the word "go." "There's no need for dates. You'll be too busy to entertain them anyway. That's what I told Drew when he asked me about bringing Sky."

Drew wants to bring Sky? He just won't quit trying to make me jealous. "But I already asked my boyfriend," I protest helplessly.

Carol's thin lips tighten. "I guess you'll have to decide what's more important then, your date or your career, won't you?" That definitely sounds like a threat, even if it was said in a tone of pure sugar.

"There you are." Austin puts a hand on my bare back before he sees I'm talking to someone. "Am I interrupting anything?"

Carol smiles sweetly. "No, I was just leaving." She locks eyes with mine. "Enjoy the rest of your night, Kaitlin."

"Who was that?" Austin asks as Carol stops a few feet away to greet Mina Burrows.

"That was Carol Ingram," I say hoarsely. "The marketing director at Wagman I was telling you about." I take a sip of my icy drink, but I can't taste it at all.

"What did she want?" His forehead wrinkles

I should probably tell Austin everything that evil woman just said. I know I need to stop hiding the truth. Maybe he could help me find a way out of this mess, but the last thing I want to do now is ruin our evening. "She wanted to congratulate me," I say instead.

"Oh." He grabs both my hands and instantly I feel safe again — for the moment. "Can you get away for a bit?" He grins. "I want to explore the hotel. Matty says there's a mirror on the lower level where you can see Marilyn Monroe's ghost! Want to check it out?"

"Sure." I take his hand and let him lead the way. As we walk towards the lobby, I have a strange feeling I'm being watched, and not by Marilyn's spirit. I look over my shoulder and see right away who is staring at me — Carol. When I catch her eye she smiles. I quickly look away and pick up my pace.

SATURDAY 7/21
NOTE TO SELF:

Teen Titan Rehearsal: Tues. 10 AM
Black Eyed Peas party w/Drew: Tues. 8 PM
Beth and Ali's set visit: Wed! :)
Stunt practice w/Sky and Bruce: Wed. 6 PM
Interview on set w/ *CosmoGirl*: Wed. 8 PM

*Schedule mtg. with Laney & Fever 2 discuss shoot.

FIFTEEN: *Kaitlin's Got the Fever*

Is Gilles Berlot trying to make me cry? Because only some-one who wants my black lash lengthening Fever mascara to run would tell me I could be shooting on a sandy beach in Ibiza, Spain, right now.

"If only you were finished filming that blow-'em-up cin-ema," Gilles clarifies in a thick French accent. "But you're not done till next week and then they say you're hosting a little movie show so you can't go then either." He peeks out from behind the camera setup in front of the striped chaise I'm poised on. Gilles is only a few inches taller than I am so I could easily stride over, grab his sweater vest, stare him straight in the eye, and ask the mustached photographer why he would tell me something so heartbreaking seconds before I'm supposed to smile for the camera. But instead I smile sweetly at the revered lens man shooting Fever's fall ads and say meekly, "This place is just as nice."

"You've always been a terrible liar, Kaitlin," he laughs. "I'd rather be in Spain too."

I'd rather be anywhere other than L.A. right now, but when Fever realized I didn't have time to travel, their location scout picked the two-bedroom penthouse at Chateau Marmont for our shoot. The suite is the largest one at the Chateau (or as Nadine described it, "this place is triple the size of my apartment!") and boasts a kitchen, living room with working fireplace, a formal dining area, and panoramic views of Hollywood. All I want to do is curl up in their super plush California king bed and sleep. My body is so beaten from the last two weeks of filming action scenes that I barely have enough strength to scowl at Drew or Sky, let alone finish out my final week on set with Hutch the Horrible.

But that's not the real reason I'm dying to pull my Rachel Rodgers wig out of retirement and jet out of town. I haven't come clean to Austin about not being able to take him to the Teen Titan Awards. Things are finally blissful between us and I haven't wanted to ruin it. I'm so torn. Do I cancel our date or do I stand up to Carol?

Clouding my vision are Mom and Laney. They're in total disagreement about how I should handle things. Mom practically wanted to call Austin herself and tell him to hand over his new Armani suit (the designer asked to dress him when they heard he was my date). "You're not bringing him," she warned. "Carol can destroy any chances you have for working at Wagman again!"

Laney surprisingly sided with me. Sort of. "The nerve of that woman telling my client how to run her career!" she barked. "That's my job!"

"Does that mean you think I should still bring Austin to the awards?" I asked hopefully, ignoring Mom's sudden coughing attack.

"Now is not the time to cross Carol," Laney said reluctantly. "Seth and your mom have been looking at scripts from Wagman for you to consider for next summer and we don't want any complications." Before I could protest, she added, "Don't think I'm going to let Carol get away with making you unhappy. I've got some discreet calls in to see what I can do. Maybe you'll be able to re-invite Austin at the last minute."

Laney doesn't know Austin like I do. He's going to HATE that plan. I know he'll say I'm giving in to Laney and Mom, which I guess I kind of am. Still, at least there's a chance they'll change Carol's mind. That's the hope I'm clinging to anyway.

"Kaitlin, you're supposed to look happy, my dear! SMILE!" Gilles shouts.

Laney gives me a stern look similar to the one Mom is always shooting me. I quickly smile and Gilles clicks away, the flash popping more times than I can count. Next I pout my lips and run a hand through my windblown hair. The whole time I'm bouncing to the beat of the mix CD Gilles made to pump me up. Even though I'm slightly distracted by my latest debacle, I actually enjoy being in front of the camera. I find it relaxing, and Gilles is so much more complimentary than Hutch is. My ego is loving the attention.

"EXCELLENT, KAITLIN," Gilles coos. Lined up behind

Gilles and his camera assistant are the Fever reps, their PR woman, and Laney. They nod their heads in agreement. "Now can you play it like you look exhausted?" Gilles asks.

I pull my bare legs onto the lounge chair and wrap the silk multicolored print wrap tightly around my bright pink bikini. I lean my head back onto the chair, throw my right arm over the top of my head, careful not to smudge the Fever Glow with You foundation, and pucker my scarlet lips. I close my eyes and listen to the flash pop over and over. When it stops, I lower my arm, lay it across my chest, and turn my head to the side. The breeze blows my curly hair over my face and covers one eye. "*Love* it!" Gilles exclaims. "Don't move. Philippe, get me my other camera. I want to zoom in for a close-up." I hear footsteps and Gilles breathing over me. "Don't move a muscle," he whispers. The camera clicks softly. "Now open your eyes slowly." The camera lens is inches from my nose. "Nice. Give me more of that." Gilles backs up to get a full shot of my face and I go through a range of emotions again — surprise, boredom, delight. Gilles makes shoots so fun that I know whatever he captures here will look amazing in print.

HOLLYWOOD SECRET NUMBER FIFTEEN: Celebrities are never as beautiful in person as they are in photographs. The truth is, we're airbrushed to perfection in almost every advertisement or photo spread you've ever seen. (Not counting paparazzi shots. Why do you think we always look so haggard in those? No touch-ups!) Magazines usually won't admit it, but almost all of them do digital retouching so that stars, and their photos, will look as amazing as possible. The photo editors I've worked with always tell me not to worry about pimple breakouts for this very reason. They remove zits, ill-placed freckles, unwanted facial hair, and even slim down body parts when needed. I've never done a nude shoot before (Can you believe I've been asked to? I'm 16!), but my friend Gina tells me *Fashionistas* took at least an inch off her butt and slimmed down her arms in her naked shots. I saw the photos and believe me, even Gina is not that tiny.

"Perfect, Kaitlin darling," Gilles enthuses when he's stopped snapping. "Très magnifique!"

Laney walks over to the two of us clapping. "Gilles, that was superb. Do you think we can break for lunch before Kaitlin changes for the next shot?"

"I could go for a little nourishment myself," Gilles agrees. "Our next setup will be in the living room, Kaitlin, so why don't you wear one of the ball gowns you've picked out?"

Laney puts her arm around me and walks me to the bedroom, where I've set up camp. Nadine and Liz are sitting on the satin bedspread, heads touching, so deep in conversation that they don't see us enter. Laney clears her throat and Liz guiltily grabs the notepad they were reading and hides it behind her back.

"Okay, spill," I order. "It's been two weeks and you guys still haven't told me what you're up to."

Nadine and Liz exchange glances.

"It's better if you don't know," Laney says.

I've heard that phrase a hundred times now. "You're in on this too?" I demand curiously.

Laney rolls her eyes. "Don't give me that look. We're not doing anything illegal." Laney's phone rings and the three of them jump. "It's me," Laney answers, turning her back. "What did you find out?" she whispers. "Uh huh. Uh huh. Shut up! GOOD. We're coming now."

"Who was that?" I ask accusingly.

Laney ignores me. "Liz, come with me. Nadine, stay with Kaitlin. Make sure Gilles doesn't try to get her to wear that yellow dress. It's horrid." She grabs Liz and heads to the door.

"Laney!" I beg as she turns the doorknob. "Was that phone call about Carol? Has anything changed with the Teen Titan situation?"

Laney turns around. "I'm sorry," Laney says as she opens the door and ushers Liz out. "No."

"This is ridiculous," I complain to Nadine once they're gone. "Why don't I get to decide who I go with?"

"I have to side with Laney," Nadine surprises me by saying. She's examining her fingernails, which look freshly manicured and painted with Liz's favorite pale pink polish. I've never known Nadine to get a manicure before — she believes in good old nail clippers. "Your career is too important to mess up over one silly date. There are plenty of other parties to bring him to. Why is this one so important?"

"Because I promised him," I say guiltily. I feel like I'm keeping Austin in the dark about so much and for once, I want to be completely honest about something and keep my word. I walk over to the rack of clothing that has been called in for today's six-hour shoot and angrily start flipping through the outfits. Nadine follows me.

"You've known for weeks that you can't take him and you've said nothing. You're just making things harder on yourself."

I grab a strapless lilac gown off the rack and hold it up for Nadine's approval. She gives me a thumbs-up and helps me with the zipper. I'm silent as I change out of my bathing suit and slip into the figure-hugging dress. "I don't want to disappoint Austin again." I answer finally. "I've done that too much already."

Before Nadine can answer, there's a soft rap on the door. "Come in," Nadine commands.

"Are you decent?" Austin pokes his head through the door.

"Yes," I laugh.

"Too bad," he jokes, slipping inside.

It's time to come clean. Nadine is right, I can't put this off any longer. I walk over and plant a hard kiss on his soft lips, wondering if this might be the last time I get to do that.

"Are you hungry? They ordered me a ton of food." I point to the rolling bar stocked with half a dozen sandwiches, a bowl of fresh strawberries, dark chocolate chip cookies (my favorite kind), sodas, and an assortment of teas (my only request to the Fever location scout).

Austin grabs a cookie from the tray and sits down on the bed. "How are you doing, Nadine?" Austin looks amazing, as usual. He takes off his royal blue nylon lacrosse jacket that says COACH on the back. He's wearing a white polo shirt that highlights his tan, and khaki shorts.

"Good." Nadine makes herself busy cleaning up my lunch. "And you?"

"Awesome." Austin grins. "The kiddies are loving lacrosse camp. Things couldn't be better." He smiles. "Thanks for helping me with the Armani appointments, by the way."

"No problem," Nadine replies, looking sternly at me. "I'll leave you two alone and knock when they need you, Kaitlin."

I slump down on the green and red striped chaise across from Austin and grip the two arms tightly. *You're the best thing that's ever happened to me. Please don't hate me when you hear what I have to tell you.*

"Hey, what's wrong?" Austin strokes my tightly clenched knuckles. "Is being a model tougher than you thought?"

"I've had better days." I smile weakly.

"Do you want to talk about it?"

I take a deep breath. "I guess you could say I messed up. Again. You see, I never thought to ask, but now they're giving me a hard time and I don't know what to do."

"Slow down," Austin laughs, squeezing my hands. "What are you talking about?"

"Carol told me I can't bring you as my date to the Teen Titan Awards," I blurt out.

"What do you mean? She's can't tell you who to bring. She's not your mother," he chuckles, then looks at me with those blue eyes and frowns. "Why aren't you laughing?"

"Because this isn't funny," I croak. "I've been lying to you. About so much." I'm too scared to look him in the face, so I focus on his loosely tied sneakers. "The real reason Drew and I are doing all these appearances together is because Carol thinks the tabloids will assume we're dating and write about us all the time, which means they're writing about the movie too, which means we're getting lots of publicity," I ramble. "What's making all this harder is how much I don't like Drew. We dated longer than I said we did, Austin, and he dumped me and talked about me to the press. He used me and I've never really gotten over that until I found you." I pause. "Anyway, I could handle the press stuff, but now she's threatening to destroy my career if I don't do exactly what she wants. And what she wants now is for me to go with Drew to the Teen Titan Awards and not bring another date. That's what she was talking to me about at the *Hollywood Girl* awards."

Austin lets go of my hands and runs his hand through his light blond hair. "So that's why Drew has been such a jerk towards me. He wants you back, doesn't he?" Austin asks. "And this explains what Hayley was talking about when she said all of the magazines her friends read say you're sneaking around behind my back with Drew Thomas."

"That's not true," I nearly shout. "That's all smoke and mirrors stuff that Carol has succeeded at doing." I think of the one-page article in last week's *Celebrity Insider* "Kaitlin Burke's Hot Secret Love Affair. SHH! Don't Tell Her Boyfriend!" I was praying Austin wouldn't see it. "I begged Laney and

Mom to fight her, but Carol is like the Darth Vader of Hollywood. She could strangle me with a wave of her hand."

"This is why you couldn't bring me to the *Antarctica* premiere. And why you went solo to that Arista benefit last week," Austin realizes. His face looks very tight and expressionless. "How long have you known about the Titan Awards?"

"Two weeks," I choke.

"You've known this for two weeks and you haven't said anything?" I anxiously bite my lip and taste blood. "I couldn't care less about going to the awards show, Kaitlin," Austin says, looking hurt. "I just wanted to go because it meant I got to spend the night with you. And all you care about is going with Drew and making Carol look good. Tell me whose priorities are messed up." Austin's voice gets louder as he speaks. He covers his eyes. "I feel like such an idiot," he says softer.

"I'm sorry," I apologize weakly. "I wanted to tell you so many times, but I could never find the right moment." The reason sounds stupid even to my own ears.

"When were you going to tell me then?" Austin asks. "The night of the awards? By e-mail?" He's now pacing the long room, maneuvering around the large clothing rack and the food cart. In the bright sun, it looks sharp-edged and harsh.

"I just . . . I was hoping the situation with Carol would . . . change." I stare out the window at the Los Angeles skyline.

"I can't do this," Austin says suddenly. "I'm trying to adjust to your world Kaitlin, but you're not making it easy. You keep shutting me out. You never tell me what's going on with work, or your problems with Laney or the studio. It's embarrassing. Sometimes I feel like a rent-a-date instead of your boyfriend. I deserve better. We both do." He's standing still now, with his back to me.

"You have no idea how hard it is for me to trust people," I protest, my voice shaking.

"I guess we agree on something," Austin turns to me and his face says it all. "I hate feeling this way, but a part of me has just been waiting for you to break my heart."

When he says that, I feel mine shatter. "What are you saying?" I whisper. When Austin doesn't answer me, tears begin to well up in my eyes, and I can't stop them.

"You want to know what really bothers me?" Austin asks. His face looks pale despite his tan. "That you're afraid to stand up for yourself. And that means you're afraid to stand up for us."

"It's not that simple, Austin," I protest. I don't know how to stop this conversation. It's like a Porsche driving in the Cheviot Hills when the brakes fail. "Sometimes I have to do things I don't want to do to help my career."

"Stop being afraid," Austin begs. "They work for *you*, remember? I bet if you told some of the bigwigs at that studio what was going on, Carol would back down."

"This is my career, Austin! This town just got over what I did at Clark. If I mess things up with Carol, I may never recover." How can I make him understand?

"You don't really believe that, do you?" Austin looks shocked. "That one woman has the power to squash your career? Stop listening to Laney and your mom and Carol and make your own decisions. What do you have to lose?"

I look down at my Manolos. "Everything." The purple and gray lines of the shoes wobble. "I'm sorry, Austin. This is my life. Take it or leave it."

His face crumbles. "Then I'm sorry too, Kaitlin." I could swear his voice just caught in his throat, but he clears it.

I don't want him to walk out that door. I want to tell him how much I need him in my life. But he gave up so easily, just like I feared he would, that my pride gets in the way of stopping him. "Please leave," I cry instead. I turn my back so that he can't see the mascara roll down my cheeks.

I hear Austin grab his coat and walk to the door. "Ask yourself this, Burke." His nickname for me is painful to hear now. "Is it worth making everyone else happy if it makes you this miserable?"

I hear the door shut behind him and I let the tears fall.

SATURDAY 8/4
NOTE TO SELF:

Who cares? My life is officially over.

THE UNTITLED HUTCH ADAMS PROJECT

SCRIPT CONTINUED:

218 INT. AIRPORT TERMINAL – SAME

We PAN ACROSS the nearly deserted terminal of the closed airport that Project XT has taken over for their operations. Mrs. Murphy and her minions are dead near Gate 26, and the converted newsstand that houses the large lab full of the superhuman serums is on fire. Donovan lies on the ground unconscious and bleeding. Carly is hiding behind an airport check-in desk, breathing heavily. Regina, the only superhuman still alive, is hunting Carly so that she can finish her off.

REGINA
Come out, come out, wherever you are, Carly.

Carly spies a crowbar lying near Donovan and makes a break for it. Regina sees Carly and runs for the crowbar too. As the fire engulfs part of the converted lab, the two fight for the crowbar. Regina gets it.

REGINA

Look at you. You're pathetic. You never would have passed
our rigorous program like I will. Just to prove it, I'm going to drop my weapon. I'll still beat you without it.

CARLY

We'll see who's the pathetic one.

She whacks Regina in the stomach with a piece of falling
debris, knocking her backwards. Regina and Carly continue to fight as the MUSIC crescendos. Regina hits Carly
in the back and Carly smashes Regina's face. The CAMERA
pulls up and we see a huge piece of steel fall to the
ground and split a row of waiting room chairs. The noise
startles Carly and she loses her footing. Regina wrestles
her to the ground and tries to strangle her.

REGINA

You couldn't leave things alone! You had to ruin them
with all your questions! You've destroyed everything Mrs.
Murphy and I worked for and now you're going to pay.

The terminal is falling apart. Carly struggles to break
free from Regina's grasp. She sees a piece of glass hanging precariously over them. Carly smiles.

CARLY

The only mistake I've made, Regina, is trusting you. But I'm smarter now. I won't fall for the pathetic best friend routine at my next high school.

REGINA

There isn't going to be a next time, Carly.

CARLY

That's what you think!

Carly swings at Regina, hitting her in the head. Regina falls backwards and we see the bruise on her cheek. Regina tries to get up, but can't find the strength. That's when she hears the glass drop from above. Carly moves to get out of the way and the glass shatters in a million pieces on top of a screaming Regina. The CAMERA CUTS AWAY so we only see Carly's reaction. She grimaces.

CARLY

I knew she couldn't cut it.

Carly shields herself from more falling debris as she makes her way through the smoke towards Donovan. She feels for a pulse. He opens his eyes and moans.

CARLY

Don, can you hear me? Can you get up?

DONOVAN
(barely a whisper)
I think my legs are broken. Get out of here, Carly. This
place is going to blow.

CARLY
Are you crazy? And face a new school of obnoxious quar-
terbacks and cheerleaders on my own? Not on your life!

CARLY
Hold on, Don. This is going to be a bumpy exit.

She drags him through a plane boarding area. We see the
fire raging behind her as she pulls Donovan out the door
to the runway and down the stairs to safety.

SIXTEEN: *The Taste of Revenge*

Ever wonder how a director shoots a major scene in a bustling airport terminal or how they fit a twenty-person camera crew inside the cramped coach cabin of a 767?

HOLLYWOOD SECRET NUMBER SIXTEEN: Even a movie directed by Steven Spielberg and starring Reese Witherspoon, Julia Roberts, *and* George Clooney wouldn't be reason enough for LAX to shut down a terminal for a week of shooting. That's why Hollywood came up with a solution for filming their countless airline scenes: They've created their own airport. Air Hollywood in Los Angeles is a 30,000 foot soundstage with a full working airport terminal that includes a bar, magazine shop, and X-ray machines as well as airplane body mockups of a 767, DC-10, and 747 that are constructed with seating, lavatories, a realistic cockpit, and removable walls for filming. Beats being hassled by the paparazzi in the arrivals area, doesn't it?

We're filming the climactic and outrageously expensive explosive scenes for our still untitled movie at Air Hollywood during our final week on set. (Notice I didn't say *final* scene. We shot that two weeks ago. That scene involves Drew, or should I say Donovan, and me walking the halls at our new high school two months after we've destroyed Project XT. We're laughing about our fabulous new lives and then we see a boy walk by drinking a fluorescent blue beverage from a clear bottle that looks remarkably familiar. "Nah, it couldn't be, could it?" Don asks Carly. The boy takes a final swig and crushes the bottle with his bare hands.)

Needless to say, with all the explosives and special effects involved in the airport battle, not to mention the stunt crew and the extras needed to play the superhuman army, our set is in chaos. Hutch isn't handling the stress as well as one would hope.

"YOU PEOPLE ARE KILLING ME!" he shouts into his megaphone. "THIS IS SUPPOSED TO BE A HARROWING SCENE AND I'M NOT FEELING EMOTION!" Hutch's AC/DC shirt is drenched with sweat. A P.A. holds out a tissue and Hutch reaches down from the camera dolly he's sitting on, grabs it, and dabs his forehead. Drew, Sky, and I, along with the actors playing Mrs. Murphy and the evil government agents (including Rodney), wait on the wrecked set for more, ahem, encouraging instructions.

"Maybe I need to meditate. Or rewrite the scene again," I hear Hutch say to Daniella, who is standing nearby with Liz. Liz seems happiest on set when she's shadowing Daniella. At least someone is having a good time.

Daniella shakes her head. "The scene is *fine*." She removes the headset covering her long black hair. "We're already over budget after the government scene you reworked. Just give the actors more direction. Nicely, Hutch. Nicely."

Instead of walking onto the set and talking to us directly, Hutch lifts his trusty megaphone again. He closes his eyes and takes a few quick, deep breaths before he chants. "People, I need to see passion. You hate each other. Feel that deeply and use it to fight to the finish. I know that won't be a problem for some of you," he adds, thankfully not looking in my direction. "And for the rest, just think of pummeling Hutch the Horrible."

I bite my lip to keep from laughing. So he knows about his nickname. . . .

"I know I'm not the easiest man to work with," Hutch continues. His voice sounds warm and friendly for the first time in weeks. Hutch looks over at Daniella, who is clutching her clipboard tightly. "We've had to overcome bad press and script leaks. That's enough to send anyone over the edge. The bottom line is that as your director, I've seen us through the dark hours." Hutch's voice echoes through the terminal waiting area. The crew decorated it to look abandoned (there is dust covering the tables, cobwebs on the walls, and all of the magazines in the kiosk are ten years out of date. Behind us are the bar and the duty-free shop, which has been converted into a lab.).

Hutch's speech is interrupted by a ringing cell phone. Cells are a big no-no in Hutch land. We collectively hold our breath as Daniella nods apologetically and takes the call.

"You've handled the pressure well," Hutch concludes, glaring at Daniella. "Now let's finish this thing and take the box office by storm like the rest of my films!"

Hutch applauds and slowly a few members of the crew nervously join in while Daniella hoists herself up on the dolly and whispers in Hutch's ear. For a moment, he looks angrier than I've ever seen him, but he quickly composes himself. "People, save that enthusiasm for later. We're going to take a ten-minute break while I attend to some urgent personal matters," he says through his megaphone. He gets off the dolly and walks quickly with Daniella to a private area of the soundstage. I look worriedly at Liz, but see she's grinning from ear to ear. A P.A. runs past me.

"Miss Mackenzie?" I hear him call to Sky, who has walked off with Drew. "You have an urgent phone call."

"Give it to my assistant, Madison," Sky snaps as she adjusts her silver bandeau top and skintight jeans.

The P.A. looks nervous. "Madison is the one calling, Miss Mackenzie." He hands Sky the phone. Sky sees me watching their exchange and I quickly look away.

"How are you feeling?" Liz asks cheerfully as she approaches me. She looks super comfy in a shrunken blue CREW t-shirt, low-cut tan cords, and Pumas. I, on the other hand, am wearing tight leather pants that cut off my circulation and a pink tank top that shows off both my real and fake bruises from the day.

"Let's see," I half-joke, scratching my black-and-blue chin. "I'm being blackmailed, my boyfriend dumped me, and my friends have been acting distant. How do you think I'm doing?"

Liz doesn't say anything. We get in the golf cart waiting to take us to my makeshift dressing room while Rodney stays behind to discuss something with the stunt coordinator. When we arrive, Nadine is standing outside the door. She looks happier than she did the day she sold her Pixar stock.

"Is she . . . ?" Liz starts to ask.

"Inside." Nadine pushes me towards the door. "She only has a few minutes before they escort her off the premises."

"Who are you talking about?" I ask as they shove me.

Liz and Nadine open the door with my name on the plastic plate and point to the couch. Madison is sitting on it hysterically crying. Nadine nudges me forward, and she and Liz stand watch at either side of me like security detail.

"What is she doing here?" I ask angrily. "It's not enough that you're with her more than you are me, but now you're hanging in my private dressing room together?"

"Madison has something she'd like to tell you," Liz explains. "DON'T YOU, Madison?"

"I don't want to hear anything she has to say," I respond bitterly.

"You'll want to hear this," Liz replies with glee.

Madison blows her nose and looks up at me with puffy eyes. "Don't blame Liz and Nadine for that article about their fight. I planted it," she gulps through tears.

"What?" I'm instantly relieved. I trust Nadine and Liz with

all my heart, but that article really hurt my feelings. I look at Nadine. She's flushed with excitement.

"Go on," Nadine demands, sounding almost like Laney. "Tell her the rest."

"I'm also the one who planted all those items about you and Drew and how jealous you were of Sky."

"I knew it!" I shriek.

"That's not all," Madison wails. She uses the sleeve of her black thermal to wipe her nose. "I made up the stuff about Hutch hating you too."

"Why are you telling me all this?" I'm shaken by Madison's confession, yet oddly comforted that Hutch might not dislike me as much as I'd assumed.

"Because she's been fired," Nadine offers smugly. "Liz and I made up this whole story about you sleeping with your ratty childhood teddy bear blanket, talked about it in front of Madison, and voila! Within days it showed up on *The Insider*!" Nadine looks extremely pleased.

"I was wondering where that story came from," I laugh.

"When Liz told Daniella what happened and how the same scenario occurs every time Madison is within earshot, Daniella told Carol, and she asked for Madison's immediate dismissal," Nadine reveals. "Liz got permission to bring Madison here to make her apologize to you before she's kicked off the premises. So you see, Liz and I are completely innocent."

"Kaitlin could sue you for all you are worth." Liz sounds

like her father, my entertainment lawyer. "And I should too for defamation of character. You almost cost me my best friend!"

"Yeah, and you almost cost me my good friend *and* my paycheck," Nadine seconds, looking like she's enjoying the confrontation now that she's off the hook herself.

I smile at both of them. "You guys couldn't get rid of me that easily," I promise.

Madison hiccups. "I'm not an awful person, Kaitlin. It's just Sky said I'd lose my job if I didn't spy on you."

Why didn't I assume that Sky would stoop that low? "You care about pleasing Sky that much?" I ask. "From what I can tell, she doesn't treat you very well."

"She's my cousin!" Madison blurts out miserably.

Nadine, Liz, and I look at each other in shock. Sky and Madison look nothing alike. Well, except for their extremely small chests. Okay, that was mean, I know.

"Our mamas are sisters. Sky needed a new assistant, and it was either this or work at my parents' whole wheat pasta factory this summer," Madison groans. "Stuffing dough into the machines is *so* boring, which is why I took this job with Sky. Job. What am I saying?" Madison shakes her head. "Sky doesn't even pay me! She said family should work for free."

"Well that explains everything," Nadine says.

"It sounds like the plot to a bad Lifetime movie," Liz agrees.

"Oh God . . . sued," Madison sobs. "I don't think I even have enough money for a plane ticket home!"

I almost feel bad for the girl now.

"You better go now while we talk over our legal action." Liz winks at me. "I'm sure security is looking for you."

Sniffling, Madison picks up her slouchy purple leather bag and snatches my box of tissues. "I'm truly sorry, Kaitlin," she says. Nadine escorts her firmly out the door.

When Nadine locks it behind her, she and Liz grab each other in a tight embrace.

"As you can see, Nadine and I completely made up," Liz says, reading my mind. "We decided to adopt your approach of handling things with Sky — we duked it out during a private kickboxing session."

"What a rush!" Nadine exclaims. "I signed up for a regular class." They both laugh. "We're sorry if we stressed you out," Nadine adds. "We know you've had a lot to deal with this summer and we haven't made things any easier."

"You guys have kept things interesting, that's for sure," I joke. "But I think from now on, Liz, you should find your own summer jobs." She chuckles. "I think it's best if I keep my personal and professional lives separate and let Nadine fly solo on the assistant front." Nadine smiles at me gratefully.

"Agreed," Liz says. "And besides, I think I've found a great job — Daniella said I could work at their production office after school."

"That's awesome, Lizzie," I begin to congratulate, but I'm interrupted by Rodney bursting through our door. What's with the surprises today? Rodney is sweating and out of breath and Nadine rushes to our mini-fridge and breaks out a Vitamin Water. He takes it gratefully and swigs it.

"You're missing the fireworks," Rodney says between deep breaths. Rod's still in his climax scene costume: a black suit, black button-down shirt, and shiny black shoes with a fake bullet wound in his chest and blood painted down his face.

"We know about Madison," I tell him.

Rodney shakes his head vigorously. "This isn't about Madison," he pants, crushing the empty plastic water bottle. "It's about Carol Ingram. Hutch just found out that Carol is the one who put the script pages on the Internet."

"What?" Nadine screeches. "But I thought that was Carol calling to fire Madison," Liz says, looking confused. "Daniella said, 'Tell Kaitlin Madison is toast.'"

Rodney shrugs. "Maybe Daniella didn't feel comfortable discussing Carol with you. The two of them were furious. Hutch was screaming into the phone and throwing lights around the set and I asked Hank what was going on and he told me. Since the coffee scene is the one fans have been salivating over, Carol's office thought it would be a great way to whet the public's appetite. She didn't ask for permission from anyone before she did it. Someone at Wagman got an anonymous tip about the leak. Apparently the Internet geek Carol gave the pages to ratted her out. Wagman just pulled her from the movie!" Rodney doesn't usually care much about gossip, but he's practically jumping up and down over this news. "I've got to get back to set to find out more."

"Could this day get any better?" Liz asks gleefully as Rodney races out.

"Wait a minute." I bite my lip, tasting the sweet fake blood I forgot was painted on. "Carol's really gone?"

"Kates, do you know what this means?" Liz squeals. "You can take Austin to the awards!" She claps her hands.

I sink into the tan leather couch and close my eyes in pain. "It's too late," I whisper. "Austin and I broke up, remember?"

Neither Liz or Nadine says anything.

"I found the magazine you guys hid, by the way," I add.

"What are you talking about?" Liz says in the high voice she uses whenever she's lying.

I open my eyes. "The new issue of *Hollywood Nation*. I found it hidden under the kitchen sink when I was looking for Oreos. I know Mina Burrows and her boyfriend broke up too."

"I knew she'd look there!" Nadine nudges Liz. "She always binges on Double Stuff Oreos when she's depressed."

"I do not!" I protest. "And I'm not depressed either." My eyes brim with tears. "I'm just in mourning."

"If Austin means that much to you, you should fight for him," Liz states, flopping down next to me. Nadine rummages through one of the cabinets and finds more hidden Oreos. She sits down on the other side of me and offers each of us a cookie.

"It's no use," I mumble between bites. "What am I going to say? 'You were right, Austin. My life *is* too complicated for a boyfriend?'" I take another bite. "Between my commitment to *FA*, movies, press, Fever, there's no time anyway. Look at Mina Burrows," I moan. "They broke up because they never saw each other. It's the curse of being in this business." I break another Oreo in two and lick the cream. "Maybe I had the Hollywood dating rules backwards. Maybe I *should* be dating other actors. At least they're used to seeing their girl-friends once a month." I crunch angrily on my cookie.

"All couples have to work at their relationship," Liz offers. "Look at me and Josh — he decided to backpack through France this month with his brother. We're not seeing each other for four whole weeks so we've been texting and call-ing every day. Nothing is ever easy, Kates. You have to try harder."

Nadine offers me the Oreo package. "Can I be honest?" she asks quietly. "I don't think Austin not being in the busi-ness was the problem." Nadine pauses. "I think the problem is that you were afraid to let him in."

"What do you mean?" I ask.

"You've always had to be careful with who you trusted, we know that," Nadine points out. "Look at what gets printed about you in the tabloids! But if you're not honest with the guys you date, then you're not going to make any relation-ship work, including one with Austin. I know you probably think I'm the last one who should be giving relationship ad-vice," adds Nadine with a grin.

Nadine is a casual dater. She doesn't want to settle down until she's at least forty because she hates the idea of a husband and kids slowing her down, like it has many of her friends from her hometown.

"But if a serious relationship is what you want, then you can't be so closed off," Nadine explains.

"I told Austin plenty of stuff," I protest.

"You didn't tell him about Drew's or Carol's demands," Liz reminds me gently. "I know those things are hard to talk about for you, but Austin's a good guy. He would have listened."

"I screwed up." I choke up. "When Austin and I started dating, he told me the one thing he needed from me was honesty." I can't cry. I have to be back on set soon to shoot. "And I couldn't give him that."

"Kates," Liz begins, but I stand up.

"It's too late," I say as firmly as I can. "I've put him through the wringer and he doesn't deserve it. I'm not going after Austin. I've got to let him go."

"Kaitlin, you're crazy!" Nadine is clearly shocked. "At least talk to him. He may give you another chance."

I look at my face in the dresser mirror. It's puffy again, like it has been for days. I use my finger to remove the smudged mascara under my eyes. I'll have our makeup artist fix the rest. "Case closed, you guys," I say firmly. "It's over, okay? Can we please talk about something else?"

Nadine's phone rings. "It's Laney," she says, looking at the caller I.D. "I have to take this. I don't know if she's heard about Carol yet."

Saved. "I have to get back to the set anyway."

"Kaitlin," Liz tries again.

"I'll see you later," I promise, rushing out the door and banging right into Hank.

"Hold up, Kaitlin," Hank says. "We're delaying the next shot for another hour. Between the news Hutch just got and what's been going on with Sky . . ."

"You mean Madison being fired?" I ask. "She must be really mad."

"Mad isn't the word." Hank massages his right shoulder as he talks. "When Sky found out Madison was fired, she started screaming. We could hear things smashing against the walls in her dressing room." I nod. I can imagine the scene. "They had to call security to calm her down, only security was busy escorting Madison from the set. Hutch went in there to talk to her and the two had words. It wasn't pretty. Hutch said he regretted hiring Sky for this project."

I've heard that line before. Normally, hearing Sky's ego get taken down a notch would make me happy, but right now I'm too depressed to care.

"Hang here and I'll call you when we're ready to start," Hank adds over his shoulder as he hurries back to his idling golf cart.

I nod sadly. Suddenly I feel very tired. I can't handle talking to Nadine and Liz about Austin anymore. Instead, I slump down on the cold cement outside my dressing room and do what I've been doing best the past few days — cry my eyes out.

TUESDAY 8/7
NOTE TO SELF:

Last day of filming: 8/9
Buy Hutch, Daniella, presents 4 wrap party on 8/10
FA start date: Aug. 21
**Ask Seth when he's sending over the first script!

seventeen: *That's a Wrap*

"If you two aren't downstairs in ten minutes, I'm leaving without you!" I yell in exasperation. There's no answer.

"I mean it!" I threaten. "Don't make me drag you down here!" My voice echoes in the two-story foyer of our house, where I'm parked with my Tod purse, keys in hand.

"Wow, you sound like your mom," Liz laughs. She and I are the only ones ready to leave for *The Untitled Hutch Adams Project* wrap party. It took Liz and me exactly twenty minutes to get dressed. We're wearing Earl jeans, borrowed from Mom's expanding collection (she'll never know they're missing — she and Dad are in Palm Springs for a little R&R), and similar black sparkly tanks. Liz has accessorized her ensemble with a sequined black beret that covers most of her dark curly tresses. My hair is pulled back in a simple high ponytail.

"RODNEY! MATT! DO YOU HEAR ME?" I try again. This is the first time the two of them are attending a film wrap as actors — rather than bodyguards or a plus one —

and they're acting like two tween girls before a Jesse McCartney concert.

Instead of the boys, it's Nadine who comes running. "Oh, it's you," she says with surprise. "I thought your mom came home early." Liz chuckles again and I squint at her menacingly.

"Are *you* ready to go?" I ask Nadine. She's been on an urgent phone call with Laney for the last twenty minutes, but she looks party-ready in a vintage Beatles t-shirt and jeans. An ebony barrette is pinning back the bangs of her smooth red hair. "You can drive and Rodney and Matt will meet us there." I tap my spiky black leather heels impatiently. I put my hand on the doorknob, but Nadine stops me from turning the handle.

"Hold up, Oscar the Grouch," she says with a smile. "What's the rush? I would think you'd be the last person who'd want to celebrate with the cast."

"I want to get there so that I can stay ten minutes and run home to my box of Oreos and my *Notting Hill* DVD," I whine.

Liz groans. "You're watching that again? That's like the eighth time this week! Would you *please* call Austin and put us out of our misery?"

"Thanks a lot," I retort. "And no, I can't call him. I told you. He deserves to be happy."

"And we don't?" Liz mutters.

"RODNEY! MATT!" I holler again. "WHAT'S TAKING SO LONG?"

"We'll be down in a minute!" Matt yells. "We're trying to

find the right scent for the occasion." There's a crash upstairs as if he's dumped the contents of an entire drawer onto the floor.

"While we're waiting, Laney wants to talk to you," Nadine tells me. She walks over to the hall phone and presses the speaker button. "Okay, Laney, go."

"HAPPY WRAP PARTY!" Laney screams cheerfully.

"Gee, Laney, you're in a good mood," I notice.

"WHY SHOULDN'T I BE? THE WITCH IS DEAD!"

"Which witch? Carol, Sky, or Madison? Wait. You don't mean that literally, do you?" Liz asks in alarm.

"I MEAN CAROL'S FINISHED. FINITO. SHE'S OUT OF THE HOLLYWOOD INNER CIRCLE. NOT ONLY HAS SHE BEEN TAKEN OFF THE MOVIE, WAGMAN HAS ALSO TERMINATED HER CONTRACT WITH THE STU-DIO. SHE WON'T WORK IN THIS TOWN AGAIN." Laney sounds practically giddy. I can hear street traffic through the speaker. "CAROL NEVER UNDERSTOOD BOUNDARIES. THAT'S WHY I LEFT HER FIRM IN THE FIRST PLACE. SHE WAS ALWAYS TOO AGGRESSIVE WITH HER PUB-LICITY MOVES. YOU CAN'T ACT LIKE GOD WITH YOUR CLIENTS . . . I'M TALKING HERE, BUDDY! DON'T TELL ME TO USE A HEADSET! I HATE HEADSETS!"

"Is that so, Laney?" Nadine winks at me.

"Laney, you never told us what happened between you two," I realize.

"SHE RUINED MY CLIENT STEVEN SUMMERS'S TOP SECRET WEDDING," Laney reveals. "SHE TIPPED OFF

THE PAPARAZZI AND THEY WERE STAKED OUT AT STEVIE'S HOME BY LAND, SEA, AND AIR. CAROL THOUGHT WE'D GET MORE PRESS FOR STEVIE'S LATEST LEGAL THRILLER IF HIS WEDDING WAS ALL OVER THE PAPERS. WHEN SHE TOLD ME WHAT SHE DID, I QUIT."

"That's so admirable, Laney," I offer.

"I HAVE MY LIMITS, KAITLIN," Laney sniffs.

Nadine and I look at each other and grin.

"NADINE TOLD ME ABOUT YOUR BOYFRIEND," Laney adds, sounding almost caring as she lays on her car horn. "STAY IN YOUR LANE! I'M SORRY, KAITLIN."

I feel a lump form in my throat and the tears start to flow. Nadine sees my face and quickly rushes Laney off the phone.

Why does breaking up have to be so painful? The nastiest gossip item or most abusive session with Hutch doesn't hurt half as much. I wonder . . . Does Austin feel this miserable even though he's the one who did the breaking off? Does he miss me like I miss him?

Rodney and Matty strolling down the stairs saves me from a full-blown weeping session. The two are blinged out in shiny gold watches and rope chains around their necks and reek of a mix of colognes, but I have to admit they both look adorable. Rodney is in a button-down black pinstripe shirt with black dress pants, while Matty is wearing a navy silk shirt with gray chinos. The sight of them makes me smile. "Are you two finally ready?" I ask, wiping my eyes.

Rodney nods. "Do you think this shirt makes me look

fat?" He models his large frame in the oversized gold mirror that hangs above the glass table.

"Would I steer you wrong, Rod-o?" Matt asks as he pushes Rodney out of the way to look at himself.

"You're a knockout, big guy," Nadine assures him.

Forty-five minutes later, Rodney is handing the valet the keys to the Lincoln and we're stepping out onto the long winding driveway of Hutch's palatial Malibu pad, which overlooks the Pacific. The front of the brightly lit, sprawling Spanish-style pink house is overflowing with people to the invitation-only event (I spotted some crashers being escorted off the premises by security on the drive up) even though the bulk of the party is being thrown in the four-acre backyard. As we walk onto the patio I can see a large screen playing a gag reel from filming; tiki torches illuminating the kidney-shaped pool, which some fully dressed partygoers are swimming in; a lavish buffet table; a DJ booth; and if I'm not mistaken, the All-American Rejects rocking out on the stone patio. A dozen waiters, wearing the black superhuman suits from the film, are passing out hors d'oeuvres and shotglasses with fluorescent blue drinks that look like the superhuman shake the baddies drank. The five of us find a vacant table next to the pool. As I go to sit down, Nadine stops me.

"Why don't you get the hard part over first?" Nadine suggests. "Find Drew and Sky so you can give Hutch his gift, thank Hutch for the opportunity to work with him, and race back to the table to hang with us." The four of them smile encouragingly while Liz pushes me away from a waiter holding mini mozzarella-and-tomato kabobs.

Sky, it turns out, is not far off. In fact, she's standing right in front of the projection screen throwing a tantrum in a red Chloe slip dress and super-high heels. Her bodyguard is trying unsuccessfully to calm her down.

"I DON'T CARE IF EVERYONE IS ON THE BLOOPER REEL!" she barks at a dude who looks remarkably like Rodney. "I DON'T LIKE BEING MADE FUN OF!"

As fate would have it, a Sky gag appears onscreen at that exact moment. It's one of Sky muffing her lines. At the end of the clip, she screeches, "I suck!" Revelers around me are laughing, as they have for all the scenes I've witnessed, including ones with me (like when I accidentally fell backwards out of a fake window, taking the wall down with me). Sky does not share their amusement.

"TELL THEM IF THEY DON'T SHUT THIS OFF RIGHT NOW, I'M NOT D-JING TONIGHT!" she yells, shaking her bottle-blond hair side to side as her bodyguard drags her away.

"That girl is mental," I hear someone behind me say. I turn around and see it's Drew. He's wearing jeans and a tight zip-up black sweater that shows off the result of weeks of running, jumping, and swordplay.

"Are you talking to me?" I ask coldly, surprised Drew isn't copping an attitude.

I notice Drew's gotten a buzz cut since we had Teen Titan rehearsals yesterday. "Chill, Katie Bear," he says, throwing an arm around my shoulder. "I actually came over to apologize."

I eye him suspiciously.

"You rejected me," he explains, "and I was insulted so I took Sky up on her offer to make your life hell." I push his arm off me. "But I didn't realize how insane that chick was!" Drew runs a hand through his short hair. "Leaking stories to the tabs, throwing tantrums on set . . . I started getting bad press from hanging with her." I don't say anything. "I know it was a lame move," Drew admits. "But cut a guy a break. It takes a big man to admit his jealousy, you know."

I can't help but laugh at Drew's horrendously bloated ego. It's almost funny to me now. This is who Drew is, and I see that now. What's happened between us is ancient history and surprisingly doesn't hurt so much anymore.

"I miss that laugh, you know," Drew says, stepping towards me again.

I groan and put my arm out to block him. "Please Drew, I might not have a boyfriend anymore, but that ship has sailed. Why don't you try being single for a few weeks and hook up with someone much hotter on your next project?" I read in *Variety* that Drew starts filming the thriller *Kingdom Come* this September.

There must be something compelling about my suggestion because Drew actually backs off. "Let's just find Hutch and get our parting gift over with," he suggests. "I doubt Sky will be back in time to join us." Drew offers me his arm. I roll my eyes jokingly and link with his for the short walk. As we pass by, the screen shows another clip of Sky. She's spitting into her hand and rubbing it on Matty's face, who looks like he might gag.

We find Hutch in his cabana, holding court with a number of admirers as he lounges on a wicker chaise. He's dressed up for a change, in a white linen shirt, dark jeans, and Birkenstocks. When he sees Drew and me, he stops puffing on the cigar he's smoking and yells, "MY TWO FAVORITE ACTORS!"

I eye the martini spilling out of his hand as Hutch stands up and opens his arms wide to give the two of us a group hug.

"Are you guys having fun? This is a fab party, isn't it?" He hiccups. His eyes are brighter than I remember and the bags are gone. His hair is pulled back neatly in a ponytail, the goatee is gone and is that — no it can't be — a smile on his face? "You two did a stupendous job. Stupendous! Didn't they?" Hutch says to us and to the group around him. I spot Daniella among them and flash her a smile.

"Kaitlin, Drew, be honest." Hank asks as he swishes his vodka tonic. "Isn't this man much nicer when he's not sitting behind the camera?" The comment elicits a roar from the peanut gallery. Hank's right, so I don't answer.

"It's true," Hutch chuckles, squeezing Drew and me tightly. "As soon as I'm done with principal photography my attitude completely changes!"

"Is it your attitude or the alcohol?" Hanks jokes.

"Sky, Drew, and I have a present for you, for directing us so skillfully," I say, trying to avoid the awkwardness. I pull the thin envelope out of my purse and hand it to our director.

HOLLYWOOD SECRET NUMBER SEVENTEEN: It's customary for stars to buy "thank you" gifts for their costars, director, and crew when they wrap a big movie. (Customary, but not obligatory.) Most stars I know chip in and buy their director a present. But big guns, like actor George Culand, sometimes buy gifts for everybody from the smallest P.A. to craft services. Other times, in lieu of a gift, stars throw, or should I say "host," because stars get everything for free, the wrap party. That's what Hutch is doing tonight.

Hutch opens the envelope and laughs. "It's a spa package for Le Petit Retreat Day Spa to help me relieve stress!" he tells the crowd. Everyone laughs.

"I have a present for you guys too. For everyone here actually," Hutch says as he hugs us both. "The winner of the Hutch Adams movie name contest." One of the P.A.s from the set hands Hutch his megaphone. "Can I get everyone's attention?" Hutch booms. I tense automatically, as if we were back on set and Hutch was about to launch into another tirade. "Everyone who wants to know the name of our outstanding film, meet in the cabana pronto." I breathe a sigh of relief.

It takes a few minutes, but everyone crowds around. I see Nadine and Liz standing by the bar with Rodney and Matty squeezed next to them, munching on wasabi chicken skewers. Sky is nowhere to be seen, although plenty of people are talking about her.

"I heard she came back, saw herself onscreen again, and practically had to be carried out kicking and screaming," someone near me whispers.

Hutch seems to be enjoying the commotion. "Okay people, this is it," Hutch calls finally. "After much discussion, Daniella and I have picked a winner. Well, what we think is the winner. What the studio decides after hearing our pick is another matter." Everyone laughs. "But in our book, this title fits our film like a glove." He reaches into his pocket and pulls out a wad of cash, held together by a rubber band. I'm assuming that's the $5,000 prize money. Silence settles over the crowd.

"*The Untitled Hutch Adams Project* will now be known as *Pretty Young Assassins* submitted by Nadine Cobb! Nadine, where are you?"

It doesn't take long to find her. Nadine lets out a deafening scream like nothing I've ever heard escape from her lips before. She pushes through the crowd and squeezes me in a tight hug.

"I won five thousand dollars!" Nadine shrieks.

Hutch hands over the wad of dough. "Brilliant, my dear," Hutch beams. "The suits are going to love this, especially the idea of referring to the film as *PYA*. Outstanding."

"Thank you, Hutch," Nadine says sincerely. "You've just personally funded my vacation to the Greek Isles."

The crowd quickly disperses after that, with some folks

hanging near Drew to hear his life story. ("My mom said I was only three when I made my first film on our trusty camcorder.") Others rush to hear the All-American Rejects' next set. As I head back to my table, Hutch pulls me aside.

"I want to apologize for saying I should have hired Sky over you," Hutch says, breathing alcohol on me. I freeze. "She had me at hello, as Tom Hanks would say," Hutch continues dizzily, mixing up the Toms. "I guess when all hell broke loose and you started to get bad press I questioned my casting choice. Thank Buddha I didn't change my mind. I've been watching the footage and you are a breath of fresh air. A true fighter. I thought you should know that."

"Thanks, Hutch," I reply gratefully. "Coming from you, that means a lot."

When I rejoin my friends, Rodney is giving a toast. "To Nadine." He holds his fluorescent blue shotglass high in the air. "And to *Pretty Young Assassins!*" We clink glasses with Nadine, who is flushed and smiling wider than I've ever seen her.

"My original title suggestion was plain old *Project Elimination*. But this new idea came to me as Sky and Kates tried to claw each other's eyes out," Nadine giggles. "That title would definitely lure me to the theater opening weekend!"

Pretty Young Assassins. It's a cool title. A hundred times better than my lame pick: *Code: Blue*, which is what Mrs. Murphy says when she realizes Donovan and Carly have stolen her computer files that discuss Project XT's sinister master plan. I guess I should stick to acting, not writing.

"Do you like it, Kates?" Nadine asks hopefully.

I reach over and squeeze Nadine as tightly as I would my ragged teddy bear, who is waiting at home on my unmade bed next to my *Notting Hill* DVD.

"It sounds like a surefire blockbuster to me," I say. But there's really only one thing on my mind: Austin. Sadly, I don't think he's thinking of me.

FRIDAY 8/10
NOTES TO SELF:

Teen Titan Awards Schedule
Tape opening film segment: Sat. @ 8 A.M.
Rehearse skit with Drew: Sat. @ 1 P.M.
Full run-through: Sat. @ 2:30 P.M.
Interviews re: Awards: Sat. 7 P.M.
Final dressing fittings: Sat. 9 P.M.
**Stop by Awards gift suite during break. Wait 4 Liz!
SUNDAY: Arrive @ 6 A.M. for makeup. Red Carpet @ 3 P.M., SHOW TAPES AT: 5 P.M.

FA start date: 8/21!!!!!

eighteen: *The Show Must Go On*

"Kaitlin?

"Kates?

"Hellooo?

"KAITLIN!"

Nadine's loud voice finally startles me out of my daze and I smack my head on the Teen Titan Awards dressing room mirror I'm standing in front of.

"Are you okay?" Nadine grabs my bare right elbow as she walks up behind me. "I've called your name like three dozen times!"

I stare at my reflection in the mirror. In addition to a minor bump on my forehead, I see my coiffed chignon, my bronzed skin, and the minimalist makeup the artist applied. I glance down at my black-and-white halter-style Zac Posen dress that has peekaboo cutouts on my hips. I'm wearing it to walk the red carpet and then I'll change into jeans and a flowy, orange peasant top for Drew's and my opening sketch.

I've got six outfit changes for the two-hour taped ceremony. "I'm okay," I reply, rubbing my head.

"Are you sure?" Liz asks worriedly. "Because you don't look fine, you look miserable."

I turn around to face them. "Don't start with me, okay?" I beg. "I've been here since six AM. I've had a full-show run-through, done two interviews, hit the gift suite with both of you — where, I might add, you both got new Motorola cell phones with three years of free service — and sat through an hour of hair and makeup. Any minute now Laney will be here with Mom, Dad, and Matt to whisk me off to the red carpet for more interviews. I can't be anything other than fine right now so let's just leave Austin out of it." My voice rises and even I recognize the note of hysteria. "It's been over a week and he hasn't called me and I haven't called him. I'd say it's officially over, so let's let it go, okay? Austin is out of my life and I'm *fine*."

"Nobody mentioned Austin, Kates," Liz says innocently. "You told us that we weren't allowed to bring him up."

"I think her exact words were, 'Say Austin's name again and you'll be fired,'" Nadine reminds Liz.

"That's right. You're not supposed to talk about him," I repeat. "I just know he's what you both were thinking about." I grab my dangling silver earrings from the dressing table to put them on, but my hands are shaking. Liz walks over and gently takes them out of my hands. Wordlessly, she removes the backing and helps me put the sparklers in my earlobes.

"Please drop this, Lizzie," I whisper, knowing Liz isn't done lecturing me. "I can't mess up the awards. I've been rehearsing with Drew for days."

In the mirror, I see Liz look at Nadine who nods encouragingly. "We're going to say this one last time and you better listen: You're making a mistake. We know you lied and messed things up, but we think you can fix this if you really want to. And we think you do."

"How many times can I apologize?" I ask quietly. "I appreciate what you're both trying to do, but it's no use." I shake my head vigorously, swinging the silver earrings. "You can't fix this for me and I can't fix it either."

"I'm surprised at you," Nadine replies simply.

I take the bait. "Why?"

"Because the Kaitlin Burke I know isn't one to give up," Nadine says, sounding like Paulo during an extra-intense workout. "The Kaitlin Burke I know fights for what she wants, whether it's a role in a Hutch Adams movie, or a ridiculous catfight against her nemesis, or a career comeback. She doesn't just lie down and die." I'm silent. "But what do I know?" Nadine shrugs and looks at Liz. "Maybe Austin, or should I say the first guy you ever really cared about — a guy who actually liked you for who you really are and not the after-parties you could get him into — isn't worth fighting for."

The three of us let the words hang there until we're interrupted by a knock at the door.

"How's my favorite client doing?" Laney asks cheerfully as

she slips inside the room with my parents and Matt. Laney is red-carpet-ready to usher me along the press line in a pair of Citizens of Humanity jeans and a fitted lace-lined black top. Mom and Dad, who aren't coming to the show ("You wouldn't look cool with your parents there," Mom explained dismissively) are in workout clothes.

"Oooh, Katie-Kat, you look lovely," Mom gushes. She thumbs the fabric on my knee-length dress and gives my look a complete once-over. Then she frowns. "You really like this better than the Angel Sanchez dress I picked out?"

"Mom, it's just the red carpet," Matt gripes. "She's got like a dozen other outfits to wear for the show. Who cares if this one isn't perfect?" Matt checks himself out in the mirror. He's wearing a black jacket with a blue silk shirt open at the collar, no tie. "What you should be worrying about is how I look. The carpet is my only chance to get on camera tonight," Matt whines, smoothing his slicked-back blond hair. "Kaitlin has two-hours worth of money shots!"

"You're right honey," Mom agrees. "Let me look at you." She stares at him for a moment. "You look gorgeous."

"You look great, Matty," Dad adds. "Better than Ashton Kutcher any day."

Everyone chuckles, but I'm still distracted by Nadine's "The Kaitlin Burke I Know" speech. Sure, Nadine's just trying to fire me up, but it's working. Even if Austin can't forgive me, he deserves to know the truth, doesn't he?

"So the red carpet arrivals begin at three o'clock," Laney is saying, reading from Nadine's daily itinerary. "There are a few *Idol* rejects down there now, but the big stars won't arrive till later. I think we're better off waiting till three thirty to bring you down. You're worth the wait." She grins broadly. "Now, you're back at work at *Family Affair* on August twenty-first, so make sure you mention how excited you are. Your mom said you should have your first *FA* script to look at in a few days, but we have some plot news already. I heard they're hiring a girl your own age to play a sweet homeless chick you and Sky befriend and eventually take into your home."

"Have they cast her yet?" Nadine asks.

"No," Laney says, "but what do we care if she only lasts a few episodes?"

"I'm going to make sure this homeless person doesn't infringe on Katie-Kat's airtime." Mom frowns. Matt clears his throat. "And I'm setting up a meeting for Matty again," Mom adds.

"ANYWAY," Laney interrupts, "plot details are minimal, but you know how to spin it, right? Afterward, we'll head backstage where you have one quick interview with Drew before you redo hair and makeup for the start of the show, which begins at five."

"Laney, where am I sitting?" Matty asks. "Am I in the front row? That's the area that gets the most screentime."

Laney looks flustered. "What do you mean where are you sitting? You don't have a seat. I thought you were just doing the carpet and then going to one of the viewing parties I got you into."

Matt is flustered. "I don't have a seat?" he repeats. "I'm the brother of the host! How can I not have a seat? Or be a seat-filler. Or *something?*"

"I'm sorry." Laney shrugs. "These tickets were hot and hard to come by. Even I've got to hang out backstage tonight."

HOLLYWOOD SECRET NUMBER EIGHTEEN: Just because you're a recognizable star doesn't mean you can just show up at any award show. For Hollywood awards, *everyone* needs a ticket, even hotties like Orlando Bloom. The truth is, hundreds of stars request tickets to shows like the Golden Globes and most are turned down (there are only 1,200 seats in the International Ballroom). Forget getting into the SAG Awards — members have to download a form seeking an invitation to *pay* for a $600 ticket.

But I don't care about tickets right now. In fact, I don't even care about the awards. Matty can host if he wants. All I can think about is Austin, after I've spent two weeks trying to forget him. But who am I kidding? Did I really think it would be that easy to get over him?

"Katie-Kins, are you okay?"

The more time I spend with Austin, the more he sees the real me: not the perfect girlfriend. But what if the real me doesn't measure up? I might make $2 million a picture, but I'm also pushed around by people and pressures that sound trivial to someone like Austin, who lives a normal life. I'm not sure Austin can understand why it's important for me to make *People*'s "Most Beautiful" issue or wear the latest $400 Jimmy Choos on the red carpet. Can he still care for me in spite of those things?

"KATES?" Liz questions.

"I'm scared," I say out loud. "I'm scared that the real me isn't enough and that's why I pushed him away."

"What is she talking about?" Dad whispers to Mom.

"I think she has stage fright," Mom explains. "Sweetie, you've been onstage before." She grabs my hand, digging her five-carat ruby ring into my palm. "This is great practice for Broadway someday."

Matt shakes his head. "They should have asked me to host."

"Then you've got to tell him," Liz encourages.

I look at my wrist. Instead of my watch there's a dangling beaded bracelet. "What time is it?"

"It's two o'clock," Nadine tells me. "You could be there in twenty minutes."

"Rodney's got the Lincoln waiting out front," Liz urges.

I grab my bag, not waiting for anyone to stop me. Rodney's got the Lincoln waiting? "But how'd you . . . ?" I look at Liz.

"Just go!" Liz commands.

"NO, YOU DON'T." Laney throws herself in front of the door. "You are not leaving the building. We have the red carpet in an hour. You can see him afterwards, Kaitlin."

"What's going on?" Mom demands.

"You said yourself, she didn't have to do the red carpet till three thirty," Nadine soothes, gently moving Laney out of the way. I bolt for the door and Liz stands in the way of Laney, as I race into the hallway.

"KAITLIN, IF YOU'RE NOT BACK HERE BY THREE

FIFTEEN I'M GOING TO HAVE A HEART ATTACK!"
Laney yells after me.

"Nadine, where is she going?" Mom screeches. But I grab
Rodney's hand and without question he jogs with me past
security, past the press line gathering on the carpet, and
straight to the parking lot.

"I knew you'd come around," he says when we reach
the car.

"We've got forty minutes to get there and back," I remind him.

"Then get in!" Rodney laughs.

The ride to Austin's house is quick. So quick that I still
haven't perfected what I'm going to say. It doesn't help that
my cell phone is ringing off the hook (I know it's Mom, so
I'm not picking up) and my stomach is in knots. Before I
know it, we're parked outside Austin's brick colonial. I bite
my lip nervously.

"He's all yours," Rodney says. "You've got ten minutes and
then I have to drag you back to Hollywood. Go get him, kid."

I take a long, deep breath, and then wordlessly grab the
car door. I hear it unlock and I swing it open. I run up the
brick walkway, afraid if I slow down I'll turn around and
dive back in the car. As I open the screen and prepare to use
the brass pineapple knocker, the red door miraculously
opens and Austin comes flying through it. He stops before
he plows me down.

"Burke," he says in surprise. "What are you . . . ?"

"Before you tell me to leave, hear what I have to say," I beg.

"But, Kaitlin . . . ," Austin interrupts.

"Please, this will only take a minute," I promise. Austin's hand is still on the open door, but he doesn't shut it. Instead he opens it a little wider. I don't waste any time waiting for him to ask me in.

"I was scared," I explain quickly. "I've been scared of you seeing who I really am. I'm so used to putting my best face forward, with airbrushed magazine covers and interviews masterminded by Laney. I'm not used to letting people see my true, unpolished, and unrehearsed self." I catch my breath before continuing. "Ever since we started dating, I've been worried about you learning too much." Austin listens intently without interrupting. "What if you didn't like the real me? Or couldn't understand me?" I ask nervously. "When Drew and I were together, he hurt me badly. I truly cared for him, but in the end it was obvious that he was just using me," I reveal, my voice breaking. "I don't think I've really gotten over that until now and I haven't let anyone get so close to me since. I should have been honest with you and told you what Carol said to me about the awards instead of keeping it from you. I should have put your feelings first because you've always been so careful with mine." I wrap my arms around myself to stop from shaking. "But what I'm most scared of is that you're going to shut this door and walk out of my life without ever really knowing how much you mean to me."

Before I can say anything else, Austin pulls me towards him and kisses me firmly on the lips. His mouth feels perfect against mine.

When we part, I ask breathlessly, "Does this mean you forgive me?" He laughs and it's only then that I actually get a good look at what he's wearing: a sharp navy jacket and dress pants. Wait a minute — is that Armani? "Austin, were you going someplace?"

He grins. "I was on my way to find *you* at the awards so *I* could apologize," he says, his blue eyes staring deep into mine. "I got a phone call reminding me of where you'd be today and what a fool I'd be if I let you slip away." He clears his throat.

LIZ.

"And a few minutes later I got an e-mail with directions to the venue."

NADINE.

He was coming to find me!

"I've been an idiot too," Austin says. I'm aware he's touching the bare skin by my dress cutouts and I can hardly breathe. "I shouldn't have mouthed off about how you handle your job. I know nothing about Hollywood!" He laughs. "I guess I was so afraid I wouldn't fit into your world that I tried to overcompensate by telling you how to do things. I think you already have enough people doing that."

"But everything you said was right." I grab him by his

lapel and shake him slightly. "I make myself miserable listening to everyone's advice but my own. And I do shut people out."

"And I'm highly competitive and I think I have the answer to everything," Austin jokes. He kisses me again. "We're quite a pair, Burke."

Rodney honks the horn. "I'm sorry, Kates!" Rodney yells through the passenger window. "Laney is freaking out! You're supposed to be back there in ten!"

"Two seconds!" I beg. I turn back to Austin. "Any chance you're up for an awards show? I have it on good authority the opening number is fabulous."

"I am dressed to party," Austin says with a grin. He takes my hand and I hold it tightly as he leads me back to the Lincoln.

"Laney, I've got them," I hear Rodney say as we climb inside. "Yes, Austin is with her. CALM DOWN. I can be there in twenty." He hangs up and looks back at both of us. "Laney is hyperventilating," he chuckles. "She said I'm to drop you two right off at the carpet. If we get there by three forty you'll have twenty minutes before you have to go back inside to prep for the opening number."

I lean back in the leather seat and smile. It feels like only seconds until we're at the Kodak Theatre.

"We're the next car in line," Rodney announces as we pull up slowly. Once we stop, he jumps out of the car to run around and open Austin's passenger side door.

"Are you ready, Burke?" Austin asks as the door opens and the bright light filters in. I hear the cameras clicking, the crowd cheering, and people shouting commands. I'm sure one of those voices is Laney.

I take Austin's hand and hold it tightly in my own. "I'm ready for anything."

HOLLYWOOD SECRET NUMBER NINETEEN: Life is uncertain, but in Hollywood, a few things are law. If you want to stay hot, don't be photographed driving with your baby in your lap. Wearing feathers will definitely land you on the worst-dressed list. Thank God, your agent, and your significant other (in that order) during acceptance speeches. And above all else, remember that the end of a movie (or a TV show, or a play, or a book) is never really the end. There's always room for a sequel. My life is no exception, so stay tuned . . .

SECRETS OF MY HOLLYWOOD LIFE
FAMILY AFFAIRS
available now

Acknowledgments:

To Cindy Eagan, my amazing editor, for making Kaitlin always sound cool (and for indulging me in my love of all things pop culture). My former editor, Phoebe Spanier, thank you for helping bring Kaitlin's journey this far. Could you please come home now? And to Elizabeth Eulberg, Little, Brown's "zactastic" publicist, who knows where to find the best margaritas in town, and the rest of incredible L,B staff — Christine Labov, Emilie Lara, and jacket designer extraordinaire, Tracy Shaw — thanks for everything you've done to make Kaitlin a success.

To my agent, Laura Dail, thank you for always having my back and for helping me look ten years forward. Mara Reinstein, for taking my endless phone calls ("Are you sure this really happened before?") and "my cousin" Amy Cohn, for letting me tag along at work and see how things are really done in Hollywood.

To my dedicated family and friends — Tyler, for napping three hours a day so that I can write, Captain Jack Sparrow, for being my lap warmer, my parents, Nick and Lynn, my mother-in-law, Gail, and the well-connected school posse, Lisa Gagliano (your students can rest easy now), AnnMarie Pullicino, and celeb-obsessed Stephanie Ralton. Finally, and most importantly, to my husband, Mike, for always understanding what I'm trying to say, even when it makes no sense coming out of my mouth.

The filming for sure-to-be-blockbuster movie *Pretty Young Assassins* has wrapped, and teen movie star Kaitlin Burke returns to life on the set of primetime drama *Family Affair*. After ten seasons of filming the hit show, Kaitlin would have thought that she could see any curve-balls coming, but with a plotting new actress on set, all bets are off. The new diva, Alexis, makes even Kaitlin's longtime nemesis Sky seem like a puppy in comparison. Can Kaitlin keep her sane boyfriend, her insane job, *and* her composure in the face of this new star power?

Dying for another glance behind the velvet ropes of stardom?
Turn the page for an exclusive sneak peek . . .

secrets OF MY HOLLYWOOD LIFe
FAMILY AFFAIRS

"EIGHT more lines than me! EIGHT!" My costar, Sky Mackenzie, charges into my dressing room, screaming like a banshee.

I look down at my script for "The Truth Is Always the Hardest to Hear," which is the fourth episode of *Family Affair*'s fifteenth season. Then I look over at my assistant, Nadine, who is ironing my Stitch jeans for my date with Austin. She rolls her eyes.

"What are you talking about?" I ask calmly. You see, as much as I loathe my troublemaking costar, I finally found time to read Nadine's favorite best-selling self-help book (*Unlock the True You*) and I now know it's not a good idea to let Sky's negative behavior get to me. So far the attitude change is working. We've been back on the set of our series *Family Affair* for almost a month and life has been blissfully incident- and tabloid-fodder–free.

"I don't usually count my lines, Sky, but I'm pretty sure I

don't have eight more than you do," I say. "I just finished reading through the script and it looks like we're both at Paige's bedside after Colby's blood is used for the transfusion."

Sky stomps over to my well-worn Pottery Barn brown leather chair and begins flipping through the script on my lap, her long hair hitting me in the face. I'm not used to seeing Sky with black hair again. She went blond for the Hutch Adams movie, *Pretty Young Assassins* (*PYA*), which we shot together this summer, but the creators of our show made her dye it back to Sara's black. Sky's hair follicles must have gone into shock from all the chemicals because my *FA* hair stylist, Paul, told me Sky's hair is falling out in chunks. Now she has to wear extensions to cover the damage. I think of Sky going bald and can't help smirking.

"What are you smiling about? This isn't funny, K," Sky snaps, her bony chest rising and falling rapidly. I can see her rib cage through her tight black V-neck tee and sheer cream tunic top. Sky spots Nadine bent over the iron and her eyes narrow.

"I'm not talking about *your* line count," Sky adds. "Alexis has more lines than me and she's only been in four episodes. Colby is a throwaway character! Her story arc is only supposed to last a few months. How could she already have more airtime?" Sky pouts. "She's trying to take over the show, K! I can feel it."

"That's what this bonding session is about? Alexis? Does this mean you've found someone new to loathe and I'm off the hook?" I ask hopefully. For once, Sky's hatred is aimed at a costar other than me, which is great because I could sure use the break.

Sky purses her full lips, which she must have plumped up with Lip Venom again, and scowls at me. "Don't tell me you've fallen for that sickeningly sweet act Alexis is selling everyone from *Access Hollywood* to craft services. I'm not buying it. I can spot a climber when I see one."

"You would know," I murmur. Oops. That's not very *True You* of me. "I mean, cut her some slack. She's only been on set for a month. She doesn't know how things work around here yet. I'm sure she's just overdoing it to try to fit in. It's got to be hard joining a cast that's been together forever."

"K, for once, could you worry about yourself instead of someone else?" Sky rolls her eyes. "We have to contain this girl's popularity before it spirals out of control." I snort. "Only two of her episodes have aired so far and already Alexis is the hottest thing to hit TV since *Grey's Anatomy*! The critics love her, the message boards are all about her, and I heard she's getting invites to all the big parties," Sky whines. "Her smug mug is all over this week's *People*! If we're not careful, Sam and Sara could be history and Colby could be the new, hot teen star of our show."

For a second, I feel a slight pang of jealousy. I mean, I'll admit, initially I was thinking the same thing Sky is now. When I read the first script of the season and saw Colby's storyline, I panicked. Colby is Alexis's character, a new girl at Summerville High that Sam and Sara befriend in the first episode. They don't know Colby's homeless, or that she's got a deep connection to their family. Our creator/executive producer Tom Pullman told the cast the character of Colby was created to cause waves with all the characters on the show for the first half of the season and then the storyline will be wrapped up and the character written off. After I heard that, I calmed down.

Still, I can't help but wonder: If Sky and I are as popular as they say we are, why do they need Colby?

I'm sure I'm just letting Sky's venomous thoughts get to me. Just because Alexis is around doesn't mean we'll be any less popular. That's ridiculous, right? I mean, having Alexis here has its advantages. Like giving the paparazzi a new face to hound. Hee-hee. "Sky, I think you're just being paranoid," I say finally.

"No I'm not!" Sky says. "Don't you remember what happened to Mischa Barton on *The O.C.*? When they needed a ratings boost, they killed her off! Then the show tanked. I don't want Sara's Beamer to flip over the side of a cliff with us in it and then *FA* to be canceled!"

Hmm . . . maybe she's right. No, no. That's silly! Think, Kaitlin. If Sky is venting to you, she must have an ulterior motive. That's what I should really be concentrating on. "Sky, this is crazy talk," I tell her. "Alexis has been nothing but nice. She's not trying to take our roles away. She's just trying to do her own." I pause. "And since when are you and I an 'us'?"

"I'm not thrilled about making you my confidant either," Sky snaps, her dark eyes blazing. "I just wanted to warn you."

I'm only half paying attention now as I reread the script for episode four, which we start shooting tomorrow. We usually shoot an episode over the course of two weeks. The writers pump out a story, two weeks later we film the one-hour drama, and two weeks after that, it airs. That's the one thing you can count on in television — a consistently grueling schedule for all twenty-four episodes of the season (we've learned the viewers hate repeats so we shoot more episodes than most). I look up and smile sweetly at Sky, trying to remain Zen. "Well, you don't have to," I reply. "I can take care of myself just fine. Thanks for your concern."

"Suit yourself." Sky tosses her hair over her shoulder. "But remember: Our contracts are up this year, K. *I'm* not worried about being renewed, of course," she says ominously, "but if I were you, I'd make sure you're seen as valuable around here. More valuable than the new girl. Don't say I didn't tell you to watch your back." Sky turns on her black open-toed Christian Louboutin heels and slams the door, knocking my newly framed picture of Austin, Liz, and her boyfriend, Josh, off the periwinkle-painted wall.

At the mention of the word "contracts," I freeze. Contract negotiations are not something to joke about. Everyone who works in TV has heard stories about stars whose contracts have not been picked up after a major set squabble or a disagreement about salary increases. Even the most popular star on a hit show isn't guaranteed to be asked back. That's why contract negotiation year is always one I sweat a little. I laugh nervously. "Sky is such a drama queen. I have no reason to worry about my conract," I say to Nadine. I silently pray she will offer me some reassurance.

Nadine eyes me over the ironing board. She's giving me her Yoda-like wise personal assistant face, which means I'm about to get a lecture.

"What?" I say, my voice sounding shrill. "You think she's right about my contract?"

"No, silly," Nadine laughs.

"Then what?" I ask. "Don't tell me you think I was being too mean to Sky!" I groan, feeling a sudden wave of guilt. I'm not very good at being the mean girl.

"That's not what I was thinking either," Nadine says. "I was thinking how glad I am that you got a backbone on that awful movie set this summer. You won't let Sky walk all over you this season."

"Definitely not," I say happily, feeling instantly better. I throw my legs over the side of the armchair and wiggle my freshly painted pink toes.

"But then again," Nadine frowns and scratches her head as she turns off the iron. Her strawberry red hair almost touches her collarbone now and she's got a green butterfly clip pinning back the bangs she's growing out. Nadine's wearing her standard set attire — a long-sleeved tee, well-worn jeans, and sneakers (today's are pink Pumas). She loves how casual assistants and the crew dress. "Maybe Sky does have a small point."

"What?" I ask, typing out a quick Note to Self memo on my Sidekick. It sounds cheesy, I know, but I've found e-mailing myself is the best way to keep track of my crazy schedule. It also helps to have a Sidekick and a super-organized assistant like Nadine who watches my back.

"I hope all this instant media love doesn't give Alexis a huge ego," Nadine says with a frown. She sidesteps the rack of shoes that wardrobe dropped off for me to try on and squeezes her slim torso around the large sack of fan mail that she's sorting for autograph requests and the occasional craze-o letter that has to be turned over to the police. "Sky is right about one thing. Alexis is in every magazine this week being called the hottest new star on the tube and the best thing to happen to *Family Affair* in years."

"She is?" Jealousy begins to rear its ugly head again and I try to push the thought out of my mind. "Wow."

"It's got to be overwhelming getting so much attention for your first acting job," says Nadine. "I mean, what has she done before? A few commercials in Canada? Her head must be spinning. We've all seen what can happen to a teen star with amazing potential when their flame burns too bright too quickly. They crash and burn," Nadine warns. "But I'm sure Alexis will be fine. The set gossip is probably wrong."

"What gossip?" I'm curious.

"It's stupid, really." Nadine looks uncomfortable. "I shouldn't be spreading rumors."

It goes against *True You* principles, but I don't care. I want to know. "I won't tell anyone," I beg.

Nadine sighs. "I overheard people whispering in wardrobe the other day about how Alexis is trying to butter up the writing staff to get more scenes," she says. "Apparently she's always bringing them cookies during meetings and stopping by to praise the lines they've written her."

"Really?" Huh. I never thought of doing that. I mean, I always thank the writers, but I've never baked them my famous caramel brownies or anything. I frown. "You think she's really trying to get more airtime? She's in plenty of scenes already."

Nadine shakes her head. "I'm sure people are just jealous of all the attention she's getting," she says. Nadine sticks the new issue of *TV Tome* in front of me. "Like this. Take a look at this article."

"Who's that girl?" have been the words on everyone's lips in the *Tome* office, where we can't get enough of gorgeous redhead Alexis Holden, who plays secret-ridden Colby on this season's *Family Affair*. The 17-year-old should spice up Summerville High, where fraternal twins Sam and Sara (eternally dueling costars Kaitlin Burke and Sky Mackenzie) walk the halls. Sure, the ratings are still stellar for this aging nighttime soap, but the addition of Alexis, as Paige's (Melissa Ralton) possible long-lost illegitimate daughter, should add some juice to the stuck-in-a-rut storylines of the past few seasons (Sam and Sara go on a triple-date with their parents? Yawn). Alexis's past seems as secret as Colby's at this point—all the show mouthpieces will say is that she was handpicked by executive producer and creator Tom Pullman for the role and she hails from Vancouver, where she was raised by her single mom—but who cares? As long as the girl can act better than that nitwit who plays Penelope, we'll TiVo in. (*Family Affair* airs Sundays at 9 PM EST.)

• •

I'm quiet for a moment. The article reminds me of a Hollywood Secret that is particularly worrisome. HOLLY-WOOD SECRET NUMBER ONE: There are a few telltale signs that a TV show's days are numbered. One is when a head writer leaves (that hasn't happened yet. Tom has been writing episodes for years). Another is when a show does a ton of stunt-casting. (Um . . . we did have Gwen Stefani drop by *Family Affair* last year. Hey, she's a genuine fan!) The third is when a bunch of new characters are brought on board . . . oh no!

"Do you think our show has gotten stale?" I ask worriedly. "Do you think that's why they hired Alexis?" As much as I sometimes complain about my crazy life on a big TV show, I wouldn't want it to disappear. You hear that, God? I actually love being on *FA!*

"*FA* is the longest running primetime drama on TV and you have top twenty Nielsen ratings," Nadine reassures me. "That's not stale. I'm sure they just hired Alexis to pull off some new plot twists."

"You're right." I tell myself, "I'm sure we've got nothing to worry about with Alexis. She's probably just trying to fit in and maybe extend her story arc for a bit." I grin. "I can't say I blame her. This is a pretty fun place to work — most of the time."

"Yeah, chauffeured rides, a fabulous assistant, a killer time slot — I would have to agree you have it pretty good." Nadine grins.

secrets of my hollywood life
FAMILY AFFAIRS
available now

Five Spectacular Stories.
One Ah-Mazing Summer.

THE CLIQUE
SUMMER COLLECTION

MASSIE
APRIL 1, 2008

DYLAN
MAY 6, 2008

ALICIA
JUNE 3, 2008

KRISTEN
JULY 1, 2008

CLAIRE
AUGUST 5, 2008

Spend Your Summer with THE CLIQUE!

poppy

hat•er \hat-er\ **noun:** person who feels intense anger and/or jealousy because of another's happiness or success.

[alt def.] Your worst nightmare.

Haters

A novel by Alisa Valdes-Rodriguez,
the *New York Times* **bestselling author of**
The Dirty Girls Social Club

a novel by alisa valdes-rodriguez
the new york times bestselling author of the dirty girls social club

From the first day at her new Southern California high school, Paski learns that the popular students may be diverse in ethnicity but are alike in their cruelty. While she tries to concentrate on mountain biking and not thinking too much about ultra-hot Chris Cabrera, Paski is troubled by the beautiful and wicked Jessica Nguyen. Here at Aliso Niguel High, money is everything and the Haters rule.

Now in paperback!

Rebecca Ferraioli

It's no secret how Jen Calonita knows the inside scoop on young Hollywood. As a senior editor at *Teen People* and a journalist for *TV Guide*, *Glamour*, and *Marie Claire*, Jen has interviewed everyone from Chad Michael Murray to Reese Witherspoon. She lives in New York with her husband Mike, son Tyler, and their Chihuahua, Captain Jack Sparrow.

Jen's third book in the Secrets series, *Secrets of My Hollywood Life: Family Affairs*, was just published and is available now in hardcover. She is currently working on a fourth book, *Secrets of My Hollywood Life: Paparazzi Princess*, coming March 2009.

For readers of the #1 *New York Times* bestselling *Gossip Girl*
and graduates of the #1 bestselling *Twilight* and *New Moon*

BETWIXT

A novel by Tara Bray Smith

FOR THREE SEVENTEEN-YEAR-OLDS, DARK MYSTERY HAS ALWAYS
LURKED AT THE CORNER OF THE EYES AND THE EDGE OF SLEEP.

Beautiful Morgan D'Amici wakes in her meager home, with blood
under her fingernails. Paintings come alive under Ondine Mason's
violet-eyed gaze. Haunted runaway Nix Saint-Michael sees halos
of light around people about to die. At a secret summer rave in
the woods, the three teenagers learn of their true origins and their
uncertain, intertwined destinies. Riveting, unflinching, and beautiful,
Betwixt is as complex and compelling as any ordinary reality.

Hachette Book Group USA   www.betwixtnovel.com

Welcome to Poppy.

A poppy is a beautiful blooming red flower
(like the one on the spine of this book). It is also
the name of the new home of your favorite series.

Poppy takes the real world and makes it
a little funnier, a little more fabulous.

Poppy novels are wild, witty, and inspiring.
They were written just for you.

So sit back, get comfy, and pick a Poppy.

poppy

www.pickapoppy.com

gossip girl

THE A-LIST   THE CLIQUE

 the it girl   POSEUR